THE DARK GOD

THE DARK GOD
A Novel of the Occult

Mary Williams

Chivers Press
Bath, England
•
Thorndike Press
Thorndike, Maine USA

v2 BD

This Large Print edition is published by Chivers Press, England, and by Thorndike Press, USA.

Published in 1999 in the U.K. by arrangement with the author.

Published in 1999 in the U.S. by arrangement with Laurence Pollinger Limited.

U.K. Hardcover ISBN 0–7540–3479–8 (Chivers Large Print)
U.K. Softcover ISBN 0–7540–3480–1 (Camden Large Print)
U.S. Softcover ISBN 0–7862–1600–X (General Series Edition)

The text of this Large Print edition is unabridged.
Other aspects of the book may vary from the original edition.

Set in 16 pt. New Times Roman.

Printed in Great Britain on acid-free paper.

British Library Cataloguing in Publication Data available

Library of Congress Cataloging-in-Publication Data

Williams, Mary, 1903–
    The dark god : a novel of the occult / Mary Williams.
       p.   cm.
    Contents: The dark god
    ISBN 0–7862–1600–X (lg. print : sc : alk. paper)
    1. Fantastic fiction, English. 2. Supernatural—Fiction.
   3. Occultism—Fiction.   I. Title.
    [PR6073.I4323D3   1999]
    823'.914—dc21   98–28859

AUTHOR'S NOTE

Although the traditional feasts of Beltane and Samain are well-known and still linger in some form or other in Celtic lands, their ancient origins are embedded in mystery and fertility rites which in the latter almost certainly involved human sacrifice.

Tir-na-Noc, the Land of Youth, and Mag-Mell, the Field of Happiness, where a minute could mean seven mortal years, represented the idealised 'other-world' and golden age of the Celts—a region of eternal love making and feasting. However, as in all magic places there was great darkness as opposed to light—horrors, ghosts and demons frequenting the phantom sphere—which was in constant warfare with the gods of the idyllic Mag-Mell.

In remote parts of Ireland, Wales, and Cornwall, connecting links with legend and history may still be found, and it is on the assumption that lingering influences of the past may be retained in the atmosphere, and deep in the race-memory, that this story has been written.

So perhaps it should more rightly be called a fairy-tale for adults than a straightforward occult novel. The theme is simple, dealing with good as opposed to evil, and light to dark.

I have set the tale in Cornwall firstly because the greater part of my life has been spent here and secondly because the grim north coast of this far point of Britain is so highly-charged with an atmosphere of past pagan forces; forces that despite commonsense can be elementally frightening to a wanderer of moors and gaunt hills when eerie twilight creeps to cromlech and dolmen.

As it is their natural habitat, natives of the remote villages and hamlets of Penwith accept this atavistic quality without fear or concern. But many a stranger or 'furriner' from up country, come to delve into psychic phenomena of loneliest Cornwall, has discovered a darker side than he anticipated, and regretted being a participant in something he did not understand.

There is, I believe, a hinterland between dream and reality, extremely dangerous to explore—a world half imaginary, half factual, where beings may walk and illusory visions take shape dangerous to the human mind.

The giants, mermaids, and well-known legends of Cornwall's standing stones are probably child-like interpretations of what was a far more terrifying past. Could it not be that in the beginning, when our earth first erupted into being, satanic powers emerged in an effort to corrupt and destroy the good and the godly? Unsuccessfully of course. Ultimately the latter must always prevail. That is not to say that certain regions of haunting are not retained under particular elemental conditions, to be conjured up at will by those sufficiently foolish and skilled in the Black Arts to do so.

Cornwall, geographically and archaeologically, seems to have a special allure for psychic researchers, and far too many dabblers have laid themselves open to evil influences through a love of mere sensationalism.

Personally I believe it is better to leave such things alone, and *The Dark God*, as I implied earlier, should be taken more as a fantasy than as factual writing on the occult.

I hope the book mystifies a little, intrigues, and entertains, with a sufficient amount of the frightening to sustain tension.

But not at midnight please. For at such an hour nightmares are at their most potent, and often more compelling than reality.

CHAPTER ONE

Rain was falling steadily. Heavy summer rain, spattering the earth with monotonous rhythm, so that bluebells and young springing bracken were weighed to the ground. Trees drooped from the downpour, yet there was no wind. Nothing but silence beyond the constant drip, drip through the bushes and young foliage. Even the house was quiet, though somewhere below Aleyne knew Lucinda was either reading, merely lazing or indulging in one of her meditative sessions—a recently acquired habit since she and Adam had moved to Summerhayes. And Adam? Was he working on his new play which had been Lucinda's excuse for their moving from town to the remote Cornish district? Or was he like herself already becoming just a trifle uneasy, and aware of an atmosphere of a compelling insidious life beneath the quiet country facade that could be at times cloying and somehow depressing?

Resolutely she thrust the thought of Adam away. He was Lucinda's now. No longer hers. Lucinda, her devastatingly attractive and rich half-sister, had stepped in, true to type, at the last moment only a month before her planned marriage to Adam and that was that. Adam had been mesmerised; most men were when Lucinda was about. The broken engagement and Lucinda's consequent marriage to her ex-fiancé had been a bitter pill to swallow, but she'd managed it. She had her pride, and had put on a bright brittle front, even agreeing to this drawn-out summer visit six months later. Now she rather wished she hadn't. Not merely because of the place. The place and its inhabitants. No one could say of course that Summerhayes was overrun by company. Between the house and the village Magswikk a mile away, there were only a few dwellings; converted cottages mostly, dotted haphazardly about the landscape between moors and sea and used mainly for summer periods or as 'retreats'. Each had its individual stamp and privacy of surrounding terrain. Yet all seemed oddly linked in a secret way, as though the little group of property owners were pledged by an unavowed bond that left her feeling alien and out in the cold. Wealth? It could be. Most of the 'élite' group were escapists from city life—secure sophisticated individuals with an imposed self-conscious yen for a back-to-nature existence.

At times the facade appeared to her quite ridiculous.

The party planned for tomorrow night for instance—'Beltane' they called it, when everyone was supposed to turn up at Manfred Hearne's place in some fancy attire as fauns, nymphs or satyrs—how really childish. And yet Aleyne was uncomfortably suspicious that

2

under the surface of such gatherings there lurked something else—something she couldn't place that was insidiously adult and slightly unpleasant, emanating from Manfred Hearne himself. Despite his over-large figure, square-jawed face and cold, rather predatory eyes under a wide forehead, there was nothing unique about him except perhaps his extraordinary hypnotic capacity of dominating most individuals or company he wished to. Women naturally felt instinctive response to such flagrant physical challenge; but men too seemed not entirely immune. Possibly, Aleyne thought, his power lay in the adeptness he'd learned earlier, as a psychologist, for dissecting human beings both mentally and physically. He was as well an entertaining if overbearing host, and a talented musician—qualities that no doubt had gone a good deal to establishing him as a latter-day male oracle in the vicinity. Although she mistrusted him, Aleyne had to concede, despite her instinctive dislike of the man, he did have talent—a 'certain capacity for the arts', as he put it, inherited from his Irish ancestry. Especially music.

There was one tune in particular he played—a pianoforte concerto in some off-beat minor key, that sent shivers of emotional response through her—a fear and longing unleashing all the pent-up physical yearnings of youth.

It was starting now.

3

Through and beyond the chink of bedroom window left open for air, the weird melody started up, faintly at first, drifting nostalgically over the beat of rain and dripping trees, gathering impetus as she listened, then dying into a sigh—a sigh that seemed to herald the death of all things before once more rising in a crescendo of life and longing. Her impulse was to go into the downpour and make her way past the wood to his house—to peer through the lounge window where he'd be sitting head half bowed, hands slipping almost motionlessly over the keys of the Baby Grand. But to go there at that moment would not be the action of a sane person. And Aleyne meant above all things to cling to her sanity—something she was determined to prove to herself through this visit to Summerhayes, by showing Adam could no longer distress her.

Adam.

Clenching both hands at her side, she moved from the window and took a good hard look at her reflection through the mirror. Pale heart-shaped face with wings of fawn-silk hair falling from a centre parting to her shoulders. Neat up-tilted breasts under the lilac coloured summer dress, large widely-set eyes merging from grey to blue but appearing darker, and a perfectly formed mouth that didn't these days smile as frequently as it should. Nothing dramatic, she thought critically, just an ordinary quite nice-looking girl with no impact

4

when women like Lucinda were about. *'Femme fatale'* she thought wrily; there was no other description aptly befitting her half-sister whose gorgeous copper hair, luscious figure and exotic features were surely predestined to entrap men. So she shouldn't blame Adam too much. She didn't; only her own stupidity in introducing them following the finale of Lucinda's first disastrous marriage.

At the time, for a brief period she'd hated her. Then, with wry acceptance, she'd turned hate into a battle with herself. And she was still fighting. She had to get used to things; to the thought of their nights together and sickening vision of intimacies that made her nerves and heart lurch in unguarded moments. If Adam had been truly happy the situation might have been easier to bear. But he wasn't. Entranced yes—up to a certain point. But taut and edgy. Already gnawed by doubts he wouldn't admit, even to himself. She'd seen it in his eyes frequently when Lucinda was near—the jealous glance and tightening of his lips as she strolled across a room towards any presentable male who happened to be there. The very way she moved—provocative hips swaying, lush and tantalising in some sheath-like dress, head proudly erect on the rounded slender neck— was itself a challenge. And Adam was no fool, no weakling. He'd take so much and no more of her insolence. Already Aleyne could sense a brooding undercurrent of danger mounting

5

between them. Something that filled her with dread.

Yet dread of what? Lucinda wasn't likely to press her luck too far. Apart from his rising reputation as a playwright, Adam's rugged good looks and the fact that he was about the most desirable male star on the social firmament would surely make her wary of jeopardising what she'd already got. No. There was no danger there. The danger, Aleyne told herself, must be in her own imagination—perhaps because she subconsciously wished it to be. And so once again her errant thoughts reached their inevitable conclusion; stick it. Stick it, and pretend you don't care. Then, in the end you probably won't. It was sheer self-masochism of course. There were periods when her whole body tightened and froze; but no one else knew—unless possibly it was Manfred Hearne himself. She'd put nothing past that man. He had eyes like a hawk—quick and calculating under hooded lids. Even through the wittiest conversation—and he was a skilled raconteur—she was uneasily aware he missed nothing, and that fundamentally he was sardonically amused by the emotional and mental little games so secretly contrived under his very nose.

She doubted whether he cared for any other living soul but himself, except perhaps that servant of his, the youth Bran, who seemed totally dedicated to his master's service. And the cat. Although Aleyne, usually, was fond of animals, Manfred's pet was the exception. The sneering glance of its narrowed emerald eyes was both intimidating and at times almost threatening. Something about its flattened ears and sinuous slinky body affronted her. She'd watched it more than once on moonlit nights streak off towards the woods, its brownish-black coat licked to greenish luminosity by the eerie light, and wondered what devilment it was up to.

Sometimes Bran followed. But then Bran would. He was off-beat, peculiar. Good-looking in his immature way, with a 'knowing' look in his dark eyes that was belied by his obvious lack of education. Some gypsy's child probably that Manfred had befriended simply to get a willing worker for an easy life and a little cash in his pocket. She judged him to be about sixteen at the most.

He had always been pleasantly servile when they met, but that very servility jarred her, because she knew instinctively it was not entirely genuine. Nothing round Summerhayes in fact rang quite true. Under the surface of the remote terrain unnerving forces stirred and vibrated—an older civilisation that had been sleeping for countless centuries and was slowly gathering impetus for eruption.

She could feel it in her bones and was frequently frightened.

But what nonsense! Aleyne told herself with

7

a sudden burst of commonsense. She was being merely melodramatic and depressed because of Adam and the incessant rain.

Perhaps though it would be still wet tomorrow, which would spare her the imbecility of having to dress up and sport about in the woods with the rest of the crowd under Manfred Hearne's stimulating encouragement. She'd no doubt everyone invited would be there—the Carsons, Emily gushing and stout and terribly 'youthful' though she must be at least twenty years her husband's senior—Yvonne Court, tall and thin, determinedly blonde with a 'yen' for high thought, exotic religions and draperies; Hiram and Rose Saunders so disgustingly rich their humble beginnings could be politely ignored; and of course Poppy Walker and Lloyd Walsh. Poppy, drifting towards the fifties, with a stage career behind her that had never properly started, was usually around whenever Lloyd chanced to be. Most of the crowd anticipated they'd marry eventually in spite of Lloyd's reputation for adroitly slipping the marital net; Poppy, though, was a little different from his former girlfriends. Apart from the indomitable will lurking beneath her fussy exterior, she possessed a tidy fortune which could very well provide the carrot for the donkey's nose.

Lloyd, nearing forty-five himself and who'd been many things in his time including chiropractitioner and osteopath, had a fancy for comfort and an easy life. Indeed, it was Poppy who'd lured him from a shaky nature-cure concern to the wilds of Magswikk. He was American by birth and quite an adept womaniser. When his expert hands first kneaded her shoulders, spine and quivering bottom, she had felt such a thrill of excitement nothing else had mattered. Love? Well maybe that wasn't exactly the word, Poppy had decided honestly. But have him she must, and would.

Lloyd of course, fully aware of the lusting libido beneath her pampered exterior, was both amused and gratified. Already his hair was thinning and a suspicion of a paunch lurking beneath his clothes. Up to date it didn't worry him. He dressed, while in Cornwall, in the current casual manner of off-beat Chinese looking silk shirts worn tunic-wise over slacks, and for social occasions velvet jackets, cut well but loosely. He was broad, but not a tall man; in fact compared with Manfred Hearne he'd be termed 'squat'. But his self-contrived sex-appeal more than compensated for lack of stature. However, even he had to look to the future.

Poppy, as everyone knew, adored him. His broad face with its sensuous lips and veiled dark eyes made most other men—even handsome ones like Adam—register as cold fish in comparison.

To Aleyne their relationship appeared mildly comic, although occasionally, as now, she felt deflated and bored, restless and uneasy by the trend of events.

'What a charade,' she thought, despising them all including herself, for becoming involved. And tomorrow evening would be worse, unless the weather broke. But of course it wouldn't. Such things always happened in reverse to wishful thinking—a prophecy which proved to be correct.

The next morning was fine, but not too clear, with a faint mist silvering the earth and undergrowth. The wood was shrouded in blue-black shadows when Aleyne got up early, and before breakfast set off with a basket on her arm to gather mushrooms. To her surprise she met Lucinda coming from the fields with sprays of greenery under her arm. She walked buoyantly, russet hair tumbled over her shoulders, cream summer dress blown gently against her breasts and thighs. They both paused with the transient early sunlight dappling their forms.

'Gorgeous isn't it?' Lucinda said. 'Adam thought it might rain, but he would. He does have such a knack sometimes of putting a damper on things.'

'Well, I wish he could have dampened things a bit more, and brought the clouds down,' Aleyne said bluntly.

'Oh.' Lucinda's smile died. 'Typical. In some

ways you're so alike, you two. Do you know, Ally, I sometimes think I should have left him alone and let you marry him.'

Inwardly furious at her half-sister's cool acceptance of her own sexual powers, Aleyne controlled herself sufficiently to say, 'Let's leave Adam out of things, shall we? The subject gets boring.'

For a brief moment Lucinda appeared to soften. 'Sorry. I didn't mean to—well, you know. But you're so serious. And it isn't worth it. No man is, not even Adam.'

'So you say.'

'Well,' Lucinda sounded a trifle discomforted. 'I'm going back. There's a lot to do. I want to look really good tonight in a mad sort of way. That's why I've got all this to cover the altogether.' She giggled half-nervously. 'What are you going as?'

'Myself if I go at all.'

'Hm. You mean you're going to be aloof and distant and hard to get, so Adam's uncomfortable. That wouldn't be clever at all. It'll be noticed and people would say you were sulking.'

'Sulking? Why? Oh yes I suppose you're right. I expect you've already let everyone know how you pinched Adam from me almost from the altar.'

'Ally!' Lucinda was genuinely aghast. 'That's not like you. And I'm not that cruel anyway. As if I would.'

11

Aleyne managed a smile. 'Forget it. Just words. But please don't try to make me play your stupid games, Lucinda. I never liked parties, as you know very well. Even as children.'

'Yes, we weren't very compatible. Funny we should've had the same father. I suppose in a way I always resented Coral—for getting him I mean. After Lyndsey she did seem so dull and domesticated. But as you never knew Lyndsey—'

'Stop it please,' Aleyne said. 'It's no good reminiscing at this point or trying to put things right. I don't blame you for what happened, and I'm not hankering after Adam one bit anymore—' (liar) '—just make him happy though. I'd hate it if you didn't.'

Lucinda shrugged, and a moment later was moving back towards the house.

Aleyne wandered abstractedly and inwardly dejected along the field path. Her interest in mushrooms had already evaporated and presently she too was on her way once more to Summerhayes.

Later that morning she realised Lucinda had been right. Not to appear at the Beltane party would be noticeable and sure to cause speculation. So she created a nymph-like dress with a ragged hem from a flimsy green summer thing she seldom wore and an hour before the festivities began, made a wreath from ferns and wild-flowers for her hair.

Promptly at seven the three of them started off for Hearne's place. Lucinda, as was to be expected, appeared ravishingly exotic in a short leaf-tunic covering her navel and buttocks only by inches. Her naked thighs curved lusciously to tapering ankles, and Aleyne noticed, with a lurch of jealousy, Adam's furious glance as she swung out of the gate, knew instinctively how his hands itched to slap her and take her in possessive love, if you could call such a primitive emotion 'love'. He was restrained in attire, wearing a loose blue shirt over jeans, with only a necklet of greenery as concession to the proceedings. His lips were set in a cold line. Aleyne guessed he detested the affair as much as she did.

Manfred's cottage stood about two hundred yards—perhaps a little more—from Summerhayes round a bend skirting the wood. In structure it was mostly Elizabethan, though a good deal of the original building had been restored, and converted for effect. Beams had been replaced where wood had rotted and a few extra installed. The exterior was washed cream under a perfectly thatched roof, and the effect against the hazy sunlight and the massed trees was of mellowed rural welcome. From the mullioned windows firelight or candles already glowed. Aleyne felt her nerves relax, until the tune started up; very softly at first, gradually gathering force as though to drain and take all emotions to its sad-sweet finale.

13

Fear, without any material cause, welled up under her frozen exterior. The three of them ambled on, almost mechanically it seemed, as though impulses of preordained fate drew them.

Then Lucinda, after a high-pitched giggle, remarked in a false brittle voice, 'What fun. Rather like *A Midsummer's Night Dream*, isn't it?'

There was a sudden cessation of all sound, followed by a sharp rattle and snap suggesting the piano lid had been brought down quickly on the keys. They went on, and a moment or two later the door of the cottage opened, revealing Hearne's figure overpoweringly large against lamplight.

He greeted them genially. 'Good, good. Glad you're not late. Everyone's here but Poppy and Lloyd. But then we mustn't grudge Poppy her entrance.' His large mouth over the square jaw was smiling, the eyes were hard. 'I was giving the others a tinkle on the Baby. To while away time—' he added with a sidelong glance towards Aleyne. 'Here, give me the coats, Adam; that lad of mine—Bran's out in the wood getting the barbecue laid on. And drinks are waiting in the lounge.'

The three of them followed him to a room, half way down the hall where he paused, gave an exaggerated bow before ushering them in and disappearing for a moment with Aleyne's thin cape and Lucinda's poncho.

14

Everyone was chatting a trifle self-consciously, with uneasy excitement, when he returned and brought drinks on a tray, from an Elizabethan court-cupboard at the far end of the room. It was a pleasant room having been converted from two smaller ones, and cunningly fitted with candle wall-lights. The colour scheme was orange and green, the over-all effect luxurious.

Emily Carson, with a glass in front of her on a small side-table, was already looking slightly bemused, and more highly flushed than usual. She was wearing, ridiculously, Aleyne thought, a kind of Columbine costume revealing thickening calves just below the knees. Her over-red hair was piled high above her stout cheeks and her smile was timid, even a little frightened and childish.

Poor Emily, Aleyne thought with a wave of genuine compassion, however outré and comic she might appear, she had pluck to stick to her guns determinedly. It must be a losing race eventually. Already her so-much-younger husband's eyes were straying. Emily must be aware of it, yet she loved him, heaven above knew why. He was nothing much to look at—rather sleek, dark-haired and ordinary. An ambiguous character with perhaps hidden depths beneath the conventional exterior. You could never tell with men, as she, Aleyne, had learned to her cost.

He was at the moment in conversation with

Yvonne, who was gesticulating wildly in a manner she supposed to be French, earrings jangling beneath her massed yellow hair, head lifted self-consciously, at an angle calculated to disguise the haggard creased neckline. What she was supposed to represent was problematical. She was simply herself, or more so, wearing longer draperies and more beads than usual, including a chain of flowers, with a marguerite behind one ear.

Hiram and Rose had made a mutual effort to appear as effective woodlanders, though the overall effect was of two chubby costermongers strayed into the scene by chance. Only Adam appeared as entirely normal, and he looked tired. The entrance of Lloyd and Poppy brightened things up a little—at least for Lucinda, who quickly weaved her way to Lloyd's side. He was attired in one of his exotic tunics and had a band with a horn sticking from it, round his head. Poppy, like Lucinda, was wearing a leafy frilly creation falling from her shoulders to thighs. She looked charming, but was aware instantly that Lucinda was one up on her and, chagrined, made her way towards Adam.

By then most of them, whether standing or seated, were savouring Manfred's particular brew of home-made wine—the 'wine of immortality' he called it, made from special herbs that had the capacity of dispelling inhibitions, taking the human mind back to

16

Tir-Na-Noc, the mystical land of youth where all life became Mag-Mell, the vast field of happiness.

There, according to Celtic mythology, a minute could mean the passing of seven mortal years.

Just a fairy tale of course, and quite ridiculous, Aleyne told herself. Yet somehow, when they all made their way later from the cottage to the wood, the queer sense of apprehension deepened in her to a dreamy foreboding unrelated to the physical laws of the present age.

The smell of something savoury cooking on the barbecue was intermingled with the pungent scent of woodsmoke. The trees filmed by hovering mist from the steamy earth were interlaced and domed above, in a pattern of etherealised beauty.

'But how delightful,' Yvonne exclaimed, theatrically enthusiastic. 'Manfred darling, what gorgeous ideas you have. I could dance and dance—I really could—forever!' and her thin arms with the bangles tinkling ridiculously, went writhing into the air with the unleashed gestures of a hypnotised snake. Someone laughed uncomfortably. Rose stumbled over a stone and was gallantly helped to her feet by Adam who muttered under his breath, 'What a farce.'

Aleyne heard him. Her tilted amber eyes caught a fleeting glance from his, and it was as

17

though the old unseen bond stirred to life again between them.

'You fool,' she thought desperately. 'Oh Adam, why did you do it?'

She could sense rather than hear the heavy sigh that seemed to brush the air for a moment, shivering through the warm night with a pulse of longing and passion renewed. Her tongue touched her lips and there was a bitter taste there.

Lucinda, completely unaware of those significant drawn-out moments, turned her head once, calling, 'Come on, you two—don't lag.'

A glimmer of light touched the satin smooth cheek-bone and one white breast half-thrust through the leafy bodice. She had captured Manfred's arm and her expression was not only proprietory, but desirous. Adam dropped Rose's arm and strode ahead catching up with Yvonne, whose exuberance had suddenly receded into a quiet almost fearful acceptance.

'What do we do afterwards?' she whispered to Adam. 'Do you know?'

He touched her shoulder reassuringly. 'Go home if we want. A few fun and games first if Manfred has his way. But it's up to us.'

'Is it?'

'Silly girl, of course,' he muttered, thinking suddenly how pathetic she was, with her youthful airs and virgin heart. A born spinster beneath her cultural-cum-hippy exterior. No

18

man probably had ever violated her innate puritanism or penetrated the secret sanctum of her womanhood. Poor, thwarted Miss Court who would never know the pressure of strong male thighs on her body—the power of setting men's hearts on fire, or the culmination of love. Against his will he envisaged how easy seduction would be and how unrewarding. He caught himself up with a stab of distaste, wondering what had got into him that he should allow a single thought of any other woman to cross his mind when Aleyne was around.

Aleyne! his senses leaped with longing, though tinged with irony. Was the sudden irrational desire for her again fanned mostly by her unavailability? A challenge stimulated by her own pride and apparent contempt for the situation?

Oh yes, Aleyne was proud. After what had happened he knew she'd hardly come placidly back to him, even if he went on his knees to her. There was, as well, his wife Lucinda. Incomprehensible, almost, that her magnetism and beauty could have inflamed him to such excess, driven him during the brief time before his marriage into believing no one or anything else counted except to possess her utterly. There were times when he blamed and almost hated her for the whole sorry business. But fundamentally he had to accept at least half the shame was his. Shame that he could have

19

so hurt and turned from the one woman he really loved and always would—Aleyne.

Did Lucinda guess the truth? Had she sufficient imagination to assess the relationship? He hardly thought so; but it was difficult to know. When he got down to basic facts his actual knowledge of Lucinda—what she really felt, and wanted from life—was practically nil. At the moment her infatuation with Hearne, whether genuine or assumed, was pretty obvious, and extremely distasteful. The man was aware of it too. His glance was sly and lecherous when it fell briefly upon the lovely face turned up to him, eyes limpid and longlashed in the flickering lights.

But then she wasn't the only one. Like a tribe of inebriated satellites the rest of the crowd were buzzing about Manfred giggling and gesticulating or frankly gaping, as though he was some pagan god with his troop of followers.

'God', though, was hardly the word, Adam thought wrily: 'devil' described the mysterious Hearne far more aptly, and he wondered about his background, what his life had been before planting himself with their little group.

The other residents had been fairly forthcoming about their previous professions and occupations, but Hearne? No. His life previous to arriving there remained a mystery; and any casual questions put to draw him out had been ambiguously discarded as of no account.

A second Alesteir Crowley? It could be, Adam decided. Or perhaps Manfred was founding himself on that professed master of the Black Arts, and trying out the trick on them all. Then why had they got so involved and impressed? Why—*why*, he asked himself once again, were they so eager to partake in the ancient festival?

Obviously the man had some unhealthy power that women, in particular, couldn't resist. He himself was more aware of it than he cared to admit, and the evening was conducive to a sense of other-worldliness, an earthy magic intensifying every moment. The whole business of course was no more than a picturesque charade, his mind insisted, but the realisation that Aleyne herself was entranced, up to a point, revolted him; and he was disturbed too by the strength of his own emotions which beneath his grim exterior were becoming each second more wildly earthy and unrestrained.

He pulled himself together with an effort, closing his eyes briefly before getting the scene into better perspective.

The light was deepening; leaves rose-touched from the glowing flames swayed fitfully in a patterned background above the silvered ground. The clear notes of a pipe sounded, gathering clarity as the tune began—the same tune played by Hearne so frequently on the piano. There was a waving of arms, like a disorientated ballet at first, until the movement gradually assumed the intermittent coherence of a united whole—of hearts and bodies servile to Hearne's command.

Then there came a sharp high laugh; an arm thrust a goblet into the air. Someone fell to his knees, hands clasped in mock prayer. Aleyne, hands extended, swayed slowly to the insidious rhythm, moving gracefully this way and that, unseeing, it seemed, of the company around her. Others followed, including Yvonne, Poppy and Lloyd hand in hand; and the Saunders becoming more plumply Bacchanalian as they pushed through the trees.

Adam was aware of a strange bemusement falling upon the gathering. At one moment he fancied a dark elongated form speeded ahead of him, touching Lucinda's hair lightly with a shadowed hand. Then the strange thing, or whatever it was, had disappeared, leaving only the confusion of muted murmuring and shifting macabre figures gradually blending into the wooded background.

Bran, in a short brown tunic, jumped impishly to attention when they reached the barbecue. His smile was wide and elfin, but the eyes for a second seemed to blaze with malignant humour, as one by one the crowd settled on the lush earth. The music had stopped, but Aleyne noticed a reed pipe near her feet, and knew it was the boy's.

The food was good, the wine, as before—heady and intoxicating. Lucinda was lusciously 'well away' before the feasting was over, aggressively sexual, with a creamy arm round Manfred's neck. Aleyne noticed him push it away once, and the expression on his face was not pleasant—contemptuous, wary, yet lascivious at the same time. Whether anyone else noticed was difficult to know. But commonsense and judgement were by then at a minimum, due undoubtedly, Adam thought through rising confusion, to something dropped into the drink by Hearne. The toast, at this point, was taken. A theatrical affair, with wavering arms and shrill excited voices raised in dedication and avowed loyalty to Tir-Na-Noc and its gods, imbued in the single entity of the mighty Hearne.

After that, strangely, insidiously, an air of peace and childish acceptance gradually dispersed any lingering scepticism, and the 'game' started, with joyful squeals from Yvonne and Poppy, and a wild urgency in Aleyne to escape and hide.

To hide forever.

To be at one with the soft grass and seductive sighing and whisperings of Nature. Secretly alone until the touch came. The touch of life—of atavistic communion before the joyous flowering. Her body ached; head and senses reeled with confusion. Dimly she was aware of hushed movement beyond and around her—the crackle of a branch, patter of feet, and giggles dying abruptly into silence. Yet the silence was potent, filled with watchfulness and waiting. Hide-and-seek. But not entirely as children played it—because the hunter, Hearne, had become a hungry god, with an animal's lust for all the wily pretence and self-display before the kill.

No, not kill, not *kill*, Aleyne's numbed mind asserted through bewilderment. A game only; this is a game. She lifted her head for a moment, searching the vastness of trees and undergrowth for someone else; the Adam she had lost, or some new Adam to restore sanity. A flicker of movement disturbed the dense blue shadows fleetingly, as a lean form swifter than an arrow streaked by her face. There was a scream; a brilliant flash of triangular snarling mouth and glaring emerald eyes beneath the flattened ears before the creature passed— feline and yet more malevolent than any normal cat could be. At the same moment the music started up again, a wailing reed-like cacophony rising to a mournful crescendo that died finally into complete silence.

Unable to move, held in the grip of an expectancy more terrifying than any physical danger, Aleyne waited motionless with her back pressed rigidly against the trunk of a tree. A remnant of reason registered briefly, suggesting, 'Keep calm, they're all here somewhere—Adam, Lucinda, Yvonne, Poppy and Lloyd. The Saunders, Carsons. And Hearne—' Oh God! Hearne! her body was icy. Thighs pressed tightly together as though carved in stone. Then, insidiously, it seemed the surface of the earth shifted a little. There was a rustling of grass, and the half-prone edging of a body towards her.

With a stab of fear that was in itself a death-in-life, mingled with a leap of painful expectancy, she saw the form arch above her, noted in a moment of clarity every line of the narrow smiling face below the black curls tipped with pale fire. The tilted seductive mouth leaned down—down—seeking hers with sweet and bitter urgency. A hand went out, her own. 'Don't touch me—' she whispered. 'Go away, you—you—'

A high laugh rose through the air shattering the stillness. Trees creaked from the sudden impact of rising wind; from near at hand Yvonne's high-pitched voice echoed with a series of short brittle laughs. 'Where are you? Who's that—?'

Aleyne forced herself to her feet. 'It's me— Aleyne.' She looked round, searching the grey air for any sign of the intruder. There was none. Only Yvonne's ridiculously clad form merging towards her through the undergrowth, hair tangled and tumbled round her bemused face. 'Isn't it odd?' she whispered. 'Really *weird*. I'm glad I've found you, Aleyne, I really *am*.'

'Did you see him?' Aleyne asked.

'Was it a "him"? There was a shadow. But—'

'Some stranger. Queer looking. Wearing horns; at least I *think* they were horns. I'm not sure. But—'

Yvonne's mouth gaped.

'*Horns* did you say? Are you *sure*?'

'Yes.'

'But who? I mean if it wasn't Manfred or Adam—perhaps Lloyd, or—or—'

'No. It was none of us,' Aleyne asserted as common sense gradually replaced fear. 'There was an intruder all right.' Yvonne's hand touched her arm timidly. It was trembling.

'Don't you think we ought to get back?' she asked, visibly shaken. 'I mean—in a place like this anything could happen, couldn't it? Those tales you hear about prowlers and murders in woods—' Her voice trailed off shakily and when Aleyne didn't reply she continued, 'The game must be over now. Manfred must have found *someone*—'

Aleyne agreed. 'Of course. Come along then.' But she was not thinking of Manfred.

When they reached the barbecue the others were all there, ambling about with glasses in their hands or seated in a half circle round the massive silhouetted form of Manfred Hearne.

'Come on, slow-coaches,' Lucinda called tipsily, her white arm taking the chance of quick contact with Manfred's. 'It was all

26

finished *ages* ago. The hide and seek, I mean. I was the first one, to be nabbed by this great— great creature. But then I would be, wouldn't I? And look at my dress—what there is of it. All tattered and torn.'

She touched a white breast provocatively. Adam's eyes glowered. Manfred's were on Aleyne.

'Did you lose yourselves?' Poppy enquired, adjusting a gap in her dress. '*We* did, didn't we, Lloyd darling?' He gave her a significant, appraising glance.

'Isn't that what it was all about?' His eyes were narrowed, the square, rather thickish mouth bland and ambiguous.

Really very like a frog. Aleyne thought, intuitively knowing, however, that his senses were still unsatiated and on fire.

Disgust for the whole affair filled her.

'Well,' she said on impulse. 'I'm really rather tired with all the scrambling about. I'm going if you don't mind, and—no thank you, Manfred—no more wine.'

'No?'

'*No.*'

'Sorry if Mag-Mell affronted you. Most of us are only too glad for the opportunity of one step, however brief, into the precincts of Tir-Na-Noc.'

'I wasn't thinking of Mag-Mell,' Aleyne said drily, with her eyes dead straight on his. 'If you must know I didn't much appreciate your

27

uninvited guest.'

'*Uninvited*? My dear girl, what are you talking about?'

'I think you know,' Aleyne answered. 'There was a stranger present at your party. At least, a stranger to *me*. And to anyone else he met, I'm sure.'

Manfred smiled with a hint of pitying derision, a gesture unobserved by Aleyne who'd turned her back. Then he said, almost in a whisper, 'I feel congratulated. My wine and particular brand of magic must have been more potent than I thought.'

Aleyne very deliberately started walking down the path—a mere shadowed ribbon now—towards the lane. There was the confused momentary sound of argument, followed by the brittle crackle of undergrowth as Adam, pulling Lucinda by the hand, caught up with her. 'The quicker we get away from this set up the better,' he muttered furiously.

'Oh, but Adam—'

'You married me, remember? Then stop acting like a slut,' he said, and was instantly shamed by the words. His grip on her arm tightened, bruising her flesh. It was as though some alien primitive influence momentarily claimed him.

Under the climbing eerie glow of the moon Lucinda's face gaped at him, blank and astonished.

Then she said in a quivery voice, 'Let me go,

you brute. Are you mad?'

His arm dropped away instantly. 'Maybe.' The tones were grim. 'Maybe we all are.'

Aleyne shivered.

'I wish you wouldn't.'

'What?'

'Talk like that.'

His hand touched hers. 'Not you, Aleyne. I didn't mean you.'

'Oh, *no!*' Lucinda cried shrilly. 'Never dear little sweet-as-pie Aleyne. Always me, isn't it? The wicked sister who crashed into the snug little love-nest—?' Her breasts were heaving violently. 'Well, *is* she so good, is she? What about the stranger in the wood? *Ask* her. Or don't you want to know.'

There was a drawn-out silence while all three struggled for composure. Then Adam questioned stonily, '*Was* there anyone, Aleyne?'

'Of course,' she said, 'I wouldn't have said so if there wasn't.'

'Did he touch you?'

'No. It wasn't that kind of contact.'

'What do you mean?'

Through a glitter of transient light he saw the semblance of a smile on her face, but it was mocking, bitter. 'I really don't know. Just a face. Call it imagination, if you like.'

They walked on moodily with the brooding unseen gathering between them. From high above, the moon shone pale and clear now.

Very far away.

Strange, Adam thought, that men had walked there and placed their little flags on its dead surface. Stranger still that on the small planet earth insidious magic lingered and worked which human beings had no way of solving.

Only Lucinda slept that night, and when she did it was as though an unknown weight pressed down on her, choking her lungs.

Some distance away Manfred Hearne sat at his piano sending waves of haunted nostalgic music through the luminous silence. As the last chord ceased, a cat screamed, bounded and streaked over the garden to the wood. There was a movement in the bushes as a shadowed small shape followed; but no one saw, though Aleyne, lying rigid in her bed, had to tense herself to stay there, with her hands pressed firmly to her ears.

CHAPTER TWO

For some days following the Beltane celebrations a curious air of unsociability encompassed the district. The usual encounters between residents, either by chance or design, just didn't occur.

Even Mrs Eliza Trewartha, who kept Magswikk village shop, seemed withdrawn and indisposed to chat when Aleyne called there for provisions. She was a small, dark, bright-eyed woman with the strong hawk-like nose and determined jaw that suggested the Spanish ancestry frequently found in far West Cornwall.

'That's all then, is it?' she remarked shortly when Aleyne's shopping bag was full.

'I think so, yes. How much?'

Turning her back, Eliza muttered a sum. Aleyne took notes and change from her purse. The woman returned to the counter, inspected the money, and placed it in the till.

Aleyne braced herself.

'Well,' she forced herself to say brightly, 'I'll be getting back.' She paused before adding, 'Such a lovely day isn't it?'

'Is it? Yes. I suppose so.' The black eyes held a sudden shrewd gleam of assessment before she continued, 'Watch your step, miss. That's my advice. Have a care.'

'Whatever do you mean?'

'Folk round these parts don't take kindly to carryings on. Not of a certain sort. That Mr Hearne now—'

'Yes?'

'Well, he's not *our* kind. We've had that sort before. And they didn't last long. I'm telling you. There are furriners *an'* furriners. There's nothing against you personally, m'dear. But if you go on having truck with such a man no good will come of it and that's for sure.'

31

Aleyne contrived a laugh.

'I'm sure I really don't know what you mean, Mrs Trewartha. We live quite a quiet life at Summerhayes usually. But if the party the other night disturbed you—'

'I wouldn't say that exactly. But things get round. Things that shouldn't happen at all.'

'If you'd explain it would help.'

The beady eyes narrowed. The firm mouth primped into a button. Then Eliza said coldly, 'I've said 'nuff. An' if you're wise you'll remember it.'

The walk back to Summerhayes seemed filled with uneasy menace. Yet it was not what had been said that blighted Aleyne's spirits, but what *hadn't*.

Adam was in the garden when she reached the house. He glanced at her suspiciously for a moment, then seeing the bag remarked almost curtly, 'Oh. Shopping!'

'Where else did you think?' Aleyne couldn't help saying quickly. 'What's the matter with you, Adam? Ever since that—that affair the other night you've been worse than a bear with a sore head. You *and* Lucinda.'

'Lucinda?' He stopped the pretence of weeding, shrugged and answered with a tightening of his lips. 'What's she been saying to you or doing? If she's been putting ideas into your head—'

'Oh nothing, *nothing*,' Aleyne said wearily. 'That's the trouble—nobody says anything. But

32

you're both pretty good at flinging an atmosphere about.'

'Atmosphere?'

'That's what I said. Perhaps *gloom* puts it better.'

His glance softened slightly. 'I'm sorry, Aleyne. But you know what your sister is—or should by now. The trouble is, I didn't. If I'd guessed half of the secret little lustings going on in her lovely head, I'd have beaten them out of her the first week of our marriage.'

Aleyne shrugged her shoulders. 'Maybe it's a pity you didn't, Adam. Some women like that kind of thing. But the idea's really rather ridiculous—' She moved past him.

'*Ridiculous?*'

'Of course. You're not the type to hurt anyone—' she paused, adding significantly, after a moment '—intentionally.'

He didn't speak or follow her, but she knew he'd got the message, and could have bitten her tongue out for the brief emotional lapse.

Once in the house a cloud of depression seized her, a sense of futility strangely at variance with the afternoon which was still and golden, dappled with a spreading pattern of light and shade from the trees outside. No trace of wind shivered the curtains through the open door. The only sound was of Adam's occasional footsteps on the flagged garden path and of Lucinda moving about upstairs— muted echoes overladen by the heavy nostalgic scent of roses permeating the atmosphere. It was as though for a brief interim, Nature's rhythm was suspended, leaving a vacuum of quiet, like a scene on a photograph or painting—the projection of a single mind intent enough to capture the imprint, and nothing more. No bird-song or glitter of wings brushing the windows. Not even the ticking of the grandfather clock registered from the hall. Nothing but suffocating unearthly silence— until the tune began, softly, insidiously, the haunting eerie melody of Hearne's creation— creeping with exquisite evil power through trees and undergrowth from his cottage, investing the air with soulless triumph.

Aleyne had to restrain her limbs to rigidity so that she, also, wasn't completely overcome. Automatically her hands went to her ears, pressing against the drums as her feet impelled her to the sittingroom window. There was a faint creaking of the stairs behind her, but she didn't hear it, nor Adam's footsteps when he went round the house to the back. Neither did she realise Lucinda had left the cottage until she saw her figure at the front gate silhouetted against the sunlight. She was wearing a long Grecian-style dress, with her bronze hair loose, licked to dying flame. Her profile for a second or two was statically clear, her arms thrust forward, almost in obeisance. Then very quietly she started moving, passing through the gate in the manner of a puppet jerked by invisible strings.

Like a wild animal scenting danger Aleyne was suddenly forced to violent reaction. The blood raced through her body again, enabling her to rush out and after the retreating figure.

As her hand gripped Lucinda's shoulder harshly, there was a sudden cessation of sound followed by a crash that could have been thunder or the monstrous finale to Manfred Hearne's composition. The effect was instantaneous.

Lucinda jerked round, shaking herself free from Aleyne's grip. Her dark eyes were wild and angry.

'Whatever are you doing? Hate me that much, do you?'

Aleyne flinched. 'If I did, I'd have left you alone to go to that—that creature,' she said bitterly. 'Perhaps I should have, for Adam's sake.'

'*Adam*?' Lucinda laughed. 'Dear me. Poor, dear Adam. I should have known.'

Aleyne, sick at heart, didn't at once reply; then she said quietly, 'Lucinda, let's go back. I *was* thinking of Adam, yes, more fool me. But of you too. Haven't you the first *idea* about Hearne? Don't you realise what he is?'

Lucinda's face was expressionless, her voice dull when she said, 'No. Do you?'

'Not really,' Aleyne admitted. 'Except that everywhere would be healthier without him.'

'Yes. I suppose that's what's so fascinating.

35

Not *knowing*. I mean, you must admit he *has* got something. And you know how it is with me—I could never resist a challenge. I'm not good, you see, or I'd never have taken Adam from you. I suppose in a way *that* was a challenge too.'

Aleyne said nothing, merely walked to the gate, where she waited for Lucinda to go through first. But before she entered the house she said with a calmness she was far from feeling, 'Let's avoid bitchiness if we can. Let's hang together, Luce.'

'Why? We never have.'

'I think we have to now. For the sake of—'

'Adam. I know, I know. You've said it many times.'

'No.' Aleyne's eyes darkened. 'Us, for a change. You and I.'

Lucinda turned away, brushing a tumbled fringe of hair from her damp forehead.

'I've no *idea* what you mean. Something to do with Manfred, obviously. But—'

'Everything to do with him,' Aleyne said with quiet emphasis. 'It's the same with me as you, I suppose. Only I try to fight against his plans—whatever they are. It all sounds childish put into words—Tir-Na-Noc, and Mag-Mell. Yet we've gone along with it, and we shouldn't have. We should have had a laugh about it and put the whole thing into perspective; seen him for what he is—a sensualist and braggart with a yen for manipulation.'

36

'Of souls?'

'Not exactly. I don't know. But he *calculates*. You can feel his mind working, even behind the bland smile. It's all an act—to get what he wants.'

'Sexually?'

'Partly,' Aleyne agreed. 'But sex is the least of it. His music's somehow—intimidating. Obscene—in a beautiful way.'

'I know.' Lucinda's voice was almost a whisper. 'That tune.'

'We shouldn't listen. It's dangerous. That's what's so frightening; to be hypnotised by a few bars on a piano.'

'Would we, if we didn't want to be?'

'Speak for yourself,' Aleyne retorted more sharply. 'Just watch your step, that's all.'

Lucinda's lips tightened mutinously, and the subject closed abruptly. They walked down the path to the front door unspeaking. Silence once more was complete, overburdened by the heavy sweetness of flowers, and a deepening sultry warmth that was oppressive. Aleyne wandered through to the kitchen where their one help, a rather surly daily girl, was preparing salad for the evening meal.

Lucinda, hearing the tap of typewriter keys above, realised Adam had come in, and was making an attempt to work. On impulse she went upstairs, and cautiously opened the door. He'd obviously got 'writer's block' as he termed it and was already pushing papers irritably away across his desk.

He faced her with a stony suspicion that made her flush and turn away mumbling an apology.

'No. Don't go,' he said quickly. 'We must talk.'

Talk? she thought ironically. What was there to talk about? What had they *ever* had to discuss, come to that? Theirs had never been that kind of marriage. Merely physical, and fun—in the early days. Nevertheless she went in and perched herself on the arm of a leather-bound arm chair.

'Fire away,' she said with uneasy, affected nonchalance.

'We've got to try,' he told her, holding out his hand. 'And it'd better be from scratch, don't you think? The other night was a farce. Obnoxious.'

'If you say so.'

Frustration filled him, with a hot desire to snap back, taking without consent what was his by right. Or was it?

He eyed her moodily, then got up and gripped her by the shoulders. 'Would you like to go back to town?' he said on the spur of the moment.

She stared at him before answering half-contemptuously, 'What on earth for?'

'You should know.'

She shook her head, forcing her eyes from the probing darkness of his own. 'I don't really,

Adam. We came here because you wanted to; now you suggest leaving, well, I don't much care for being ushered from pillar to post just because of some silly mood of yours—'

'Is it a mood? Is it?' His fingers bit into her flesh painfully. 'That man Hearne—'

She shook herself free, laughing, but without humour, 'Oh Adam—*really*. Him. What's he got to do with it?'

'That's what I'd like to know,' he answered heavily. 'Good God, I should think by now the whole neighbourhood's noticed. And I won't be cuckolded, Luce. Remember that. Do you understand?'

'Oh yes, perfectly. And you might do a bit of remembering yourself too. Aleyne, for instance—'

'What about Aleyne?' He swung her round again, more harshly than he meant. Her eyes widened, she attempted to break away, but almost before she knew it, his lips were on her mouth, one hand cupping a breast as her neck arched backwards, releasing the rich hair in a copper stream over her shoulders and spine.

He laid her on the sofa purposefully, undoing the flimsy dress and underwear, until she lay staring at him desiring and yet hating at the same time, pulses throbbing with fear and expectation. Then as his body bore down on her, the light momentarily darkened. All air, for that brief interim seemed drained from her lungs. With a choking sense of terror she was aware of a shadowed shape hovering above and around, encompassing the atmosphere with spreading malevolent evil. There was a scream of torment that could have been her own, or of that other encroaching entity—the sudden flare of two reddened eyes, and streaking half-glimpsed form as it sprang and dived towards the window. Then, suddenly, an acute icy chill.

Adam jumped up, wiping the perspiration from his neck and forehead.

'There was no need for that,' he said, 'Sorry I—' His voice was thick with anger and humiliation.

Lucinda lifted one hand objecting. 'But Adam, I didn't—there was something *there*. Didn't you see? Something—'

Her voice faded into bewilderment.

He laughed.

'Don't lie, Lucinda. I've got the message.'

'I wasn't lying. That sound—'

'The thunder, you mean? Poor girl. Still, a good excuse.'

'Thunder?'

As she echoed the word, there was a flash of lightning followed almost immediately by a distinct low rumble from the west. 'But it wasn't that,' she whispered. 'Believe me, please, Adam.'

He shrugged, and went to the mirror, adjusting his tie and raking a comb through his hair. Then he walked to the door, paused

40

there, turned and said quietly, 'Get dressed, Lucinda. You look a mess.'

When the door had closed, she lay for a few minutes revisualising the scene. Was it true what he'd implied? Was she a weakling, or mad?

The thought was terrifying, but not half so terrifying as the truth. And of that she was certain, it was not thunder she'd heard. And the shadow, the horror had been there.

CHAPTER THREE

Yvonne was next to see the shadow.

It happened a fortnight later, following two days of light summer rain that had freshened the earth and reduced the memory of Beltane to proper proportions. Those who thought of it at all considered the whole idea no more than a childish prank. The rest dismissed it wilfully, but with some discomfort, as not worth remembering.

The tempo and life-style of the little group assumed its normal pattern of three nights a week visiting each other's houses for drinks and bridge. Days were spent bathing or idling about in the cove a quarter of a mile away where a path led from the cliffs down a ravine to the beach.

On Saturdays Adam and Lloyd generally

went off for a round of golf on the links some distance the other side of the village. The womenfolk took the opportunity mostly of driving to Penzance for shopping or hair-dos, except for Rose who was grateful for the chance of burying herself in the kitchen. She tried desperately, for Hiram's sake, to adjust herself to the new fashionable routine of smart talk and what seemed to her secretly an artificial and frightening existence. No one could have guessed the terrors lurking beneath her placid exterior; not even Hiram, although he sensed at week-ends a restoration of their old easy relationship, when new-fangled notions could be shrugged off as a bit of a laugh. These periods left them sane. But Yvonne was a different matter.

Yvonne did not care for Penzance, and had a positive phobia against cars because she had once been involved in a minor accident. Her whole being therefore revolved round the district; her own cottage in particular, which lay not more than a hundred yards from Manfred Hearne's, on the moorland side. The small building was less modernised than the rest, granite-faced, but with blue paint, because blue, she considered, denoted an aura of peace, and provided the right background for her temperament. Being, as she professed, astrologically, a Cancerian, suitable surroundings were essential to her sensitive temperament. The interior of the cottage was similarly harmonious. Whereas the Carsons and Saunders had resorted to chrome interspersed with light oak, and a few pieces of modern sculpture carefully placed in corners designed on abstract lines, Yvonne had clung to cherished family antiques with Liberty print hangings and curtains in varied shades of her favourite blue. The lounge downstairs was large and comfortable, converted from what once had been two small rooms. The kitchen at the back was a mere cubby hole, but conveniently fitted with necessary equipment.

Her particular sanctum was a covered-in veranda, where she could indulge herself in her particular craft—hand-weaving. Mostly she worked for pleasure; but whenever her limited income took a rather downward turn she had no difficulty in placing her fine scarves, tableware and skirts, commercially. There was one thing she loathed above cars, even: one of those horrid letters from the bank saying she was overdrawn, and suggesting it would be much appreciated if she could remedy the deficiency as soon as possible.

On that certain Saturday afternoon, however, there was no bank niggle, no outstanding bills to fret over. Everything seemed as near perfect as one of her highly strung temperament could expect. So she settled to a period of weaving in order to complete a set of table mats, and broke off after an hour's work, intending to resume following a cup of tea. Then, lured by the calm summer day, and on the pretext that she needed ragwort for her next dyeing session, she set off with a large Cellophane sack for Crowcarne field—a wild deserted patch of ground lying on the western side of the wood, past Manfred Hearne's cottage.

As usual, long earrings jangled beneath the fuzzed hair. Only the tips of sandals peered beneath her long hand-woven skirt. Two bracelets dangled on one thin wrist. In the slanting brilliant light dappling the ground through the motionless trees, she had a slightly grotesque elfin appearance; insubstantial almost, as though created from the elemental scene. Yet no sense of evil lurked there; only, to her heightened fancy, a queer feeling of youthful happiness that made her want to leap and laugh suddenly in a manner quite unbefitting her years.

Hearne's cottage was completely quiet when she passed. No haunting echo of his nostalgic concerto broke the utter silence. No movement of his large face behind the window or great form lurking in the porch. She flung one glance, then hurried on, head half-averted, repressing a wild desire to giggle, though she had no idea why.

She hurried towards the slight dip, where the massed flashing gold of ragwort flamed brilliant against the dull green. And then, unexpectedly, the shadow fell—freezing her

44

mind to a slow welling up of fear. Automatically her footsteps halted as the darkness—'thing'—whatever it was, descended like an immense shroud over her head, eyes, and whole body, encompassing the surrounding terrain into a terrifying preknowledge of ultimate doom and extinction.

Though her sight was blurred, she could distinguish the menace of an immense form emanating—a shape bearing no relationship to anything human, but so incredibly evil that sickness rose in her. Unknowingly one hand reached out to the empty air. Her figure swayed, and a high scream dying into laughter pierced the silence. She dropped the bag, and turned, clasping her own throat automatically.

For a second she had a brief sight of eyes watching her malignantly from the huddled trees—fancied a slim figure, black as ebony, darted into the tangled shadows. Then, very slowly, the abomination lifted. Sunlight filtered across the ground, dispelling the darkness.

From static immobility her whole body started trembling violently. The blood coursed through her veins again, and, forgetting the bag, she rushed wildly back the way she had come, towards Manfred Hearne's cottage. Manfred—she thought hysterically, he will help—he'll save me. Manfred—Manfred—

He was standing near his gate when she got there, his square face expressionless except for a slight lift of the brows above the wary eyes.

She rushed towards him flinging herself against his chest, unconscious of the slight contemptuous twist of his lips.

'Oh—oh,' she gasped, 'Mr Hearne—please—'

'My dear Miss Court. Yvonne, whatever's the matter? Come now, come along, we can't have this—'

He half led, half dragged her into the cottage; took her through to the lounge and eased her into an armchair. She sank back gratefully, closed her eyes briefly while the shivering started all over again. He regarded her speculatively for a moment then fetched her a drink—not his renowned 'special brew', but something considerably sharper. In a few seconds a wave of faint colour stained her thin cheeks. Her breathing eased, and she managed an artificial laugh.

'What must you think of me? It seems so absurd. And yet—'

'Yes?'

'There was something *out* there,' she continued, with a look of dull terror clouding her eyes again. 'Something I can't explain. Oh—' her voice rose to a shriek as the lean form of Manfred's cat streaked from some unknown hiding place to a chair directly opposite. Its blazing emerald eyes regarded her maliciously, the upper lip of its triangular face lifted in a sneer.

46

Manfred laughed. 'Perhaps it was Sam,' he said lightly. 'But Sam's really quite amenable provided he's not scared.'

Yvonne swallowed nervously. '*That* thing scared—?' Her tones were shrill, hysterical.

Manfred touched her shoulder lightly. 'Now really! you mustn't regard Sam as a "*thing*". He's a very intelligent animal.' There was a pause in which his eyes held hers hypnotically—strange molten eyes with dilated pupils contracting suddenly to mere pin-points of darkness. And as she stared up at him it was as though her very spirit faltered and was drawn back to the furthermost recesses of childhood and beyond that to the womb—in which she struggled as some rejected entity for life. Her parents had never wanted her, of course. They had been elderly and obsessed by their own sterile creative efforts in literary and musical spheres. She had been a mistake and a burden; an imposition to be born and disciplined against intrusion. Nothing in her youth had been joyful, and under Manfred's compelling gaze it was as though the past bleak image of her life was reborn in bitter accusation.

'No—no—' she whispered. 'Go away—'

Hearne's fingers traced her neck gently, skilfully unbuttoning the neck of her blouse. Then he eased the flimsy material over her shoulders to the waist, revealing the unlovely cotton vest with the built up straps. This he pulled down and stood regarding her for a moment before placing both hands on her waist. Her jaw dropped as her senses stirred not in fear this time, but pleasure. Very softly and slowly the expert fingers slid to the small breasts, encasing them firmly. The contact was brief, but sufficient to stimulate all the repressed instincts of her virgin years. Her thin figure swayed involuntarily towards him. Her eyes closed.

'Turn round, Miss Court,' he whispered in her ear.

She obeyed blindly, and felt his touch on her spine, tracing each vertebra with the subtle softness of a butterfly's wings against her dry skin. Small tremors of delight brought the blood to her veins. She sighed, stiffened, then relaxed into anticipatory desire as the large palms reached the too thin buttocks. There was a momentary increase of pressure, followed by a repetition of the process—a caressing, stroking motion down the whole of her back, while her heart quickened wildly as any girl's. Then he released her abruptly, saying in slightly thickened though practical tones, 'There now. A little manipulation—and the terror's gone I hope—?'

'Oh Mr Hearne—Manfred—' she lifted both hands as though in supplication. 'You are so—how can I thank you?'

His mouth smiled beneath the hard eyes. Jerking his jacket into place round the

48

shoulders he said, 'We'll keep it as our little secret, shall we? And anytime you're frightened you must remember nothing can harm you. You *mustn't doubt* life, Yvonne. In those two little hands of yours—that yearning terrified feminine mind, you have the capacity of all things if you once learn to enter Tir-Na-Noc and Mag-Mell. Remember that, and don't forget your meditation—'

His voice paused briefly as her startled eyes widened. 'Promise me now;' he took her hand once more, thinking how like a frightened fox she looked with her pointed nose and quivering mouth.

She nodded, and a sigh of relief released the tension of her large frame. He knew he had won. She was his whenever he wished it; his subject—almost his familiar. Not a particularly ravishing conquest, but the virginal Miss Court would doubtless have her uses later, when he was out for richer prey. So he was careful to keep the game up, and before she left saw she was re-fortified by a glass of his own brew.

As Yvonne went through the gate, the sun enveloped her in a spreading glow of well-being and warmth. Her mind and senses were dancing. It seemed to her that the very May trees sang as a frail wind scurried through the air, shaking the blossoms in heady sweetness. What a wonderful man, she thought, when she reached her cottage and wandered round to her veranda. How kind he had been but so exciting. Unconsciously one hand strayed to the back of her neck and down a shoulder to the curve of the thin breast he'd caressed. He was a healer, there was no doubt of that; he had not only subdued her terrors, but given her new faith in herself with the conviction that she was not, after all, so very old.

Old? How could she be—when Tir-Na-Noc waited in the dark wood, and the wondrous Mag-Mell ruled over by the great Manfred Hearne, her friend?

It was only later, when evening came, that her jubilation receded into sudden overwhelming tiredness burdened with a heavy sense of unreality. The old feeling of guilt returned. She had behaved like any unprincipled wanton she told herself ruthlessly, letting Manfred touch her where no male hands had ever strayed before. At the same time she was aware that it was only the beginning. If he wished it again she would not—*could* not deny him. The knowledge troubled her; troubled her so much that presently she flung herself on the bed with great shuddering sobs tearing her body.

She did not see the pointed dark face peering at her window from the elder tree outside, or sudden speeding through the green twilight of a slim male form. Neither did she notice the elongated shadows creeping across her carpet, fantastically suggestive of horned head and claws. She did not look up until the

50

insidious echo of Manfred's tune drifted nostalgically through the evening air, gathering momentum while the rising wind soared through branches and rustling undergrowth. At that point, impelled by a force beyond her own will or reason, she got up and went to the window.

A woman was walking half-gliding down the track towards Hearne's cottage. She had long tumbled hair, and her arms were stretched out, above the briefly silhouetted breasts. A surge of hatred flooded Yvonne's being, her normally pale face became suffused with dull throbbing crimson. For a second or two she was murderous in spirit. Then as quickly the irrational mood changed.

'Forgive me,' she muttered through shaking jaws. 'God forgive me.' But whether God heard or not made no difference. She knew she was already lost and beyond any human or spiritual help.

CHAPTER FOUR

During the next few days Yvonne managed to persuade herself she had mistaken the identity of the female figure passing her gate. The light had been queer, with a greenish tone that could be distorting under certain conditions. And even if it *had* been Lucinda there was no proof she was visiting Manfred. Besides, she thought, with a thrill of memory—she wasn't his type. Far too brash; obviously he preferred a woman of refinement such as herself.

All the same, she did not allow herself to become complacent, and was forever on the watch—so absorbed in her own affairs, her bemused air became noticeable.

'Poor old Yvonne seems to be going completely ga-ga,' Poppy told Lloyd reflectively one evening. 'If you ask me she's nuts about our friend Manfred.'

Lloyd, sprawled in her most comfortable armchair, with a half bottle of scotch already consumed, threw a lazy oblique glance at her before remarking with a wry touch of humour, 'And what about you?'

'Me?' Poppy swung round, laughing. A beam of dying sunlight caught her face cruelly, revealing harshly what she generally contrived so well to hide—her age. Her expression, though amused, was ironic; and red, Lloyd thought, was not her colour. Nevertheless her small deceits didn't worry him. He'd long been aware she was no chicken. And he admired her sporting instinct, though he wished she'd soften up occasionally. A woman so hard to get was an anachronism. But then the clever type often were. She was out to marry him, of course. Well, he probably would, eventually, and when that happened he'd teach her a thing or two. He and Manfred had one thing in

52

common—an understanding of the opposite sex.

'Yes, *you*,' he heard himself saying. 'Don't try that one on me, darling. I know *you* and I know men.'

'I can assure you,' Poppy said coldly, 'Manfred hasn't the slightest interest in me, or I in him.'

'Only because *I* happen to be on the horizon,' Lloyd said.

'Yes,' Poppy leaned over, slipping an arm round his shoulders. 'That's true. Come to think of it you *are* a bit alike. Manipulators, both of you.'

He laughed throatily, and pulled her down on to his knee.

'When is it going to be?'

'What?'

'You know what. *When*, Poppy?'

She jumped up pushing the tumbled hair from her forehead. Then standing very erectly, with her eyes suddenly rather cold on his face, she said, 'That's up to you, Lloyd. In some ways I'm not very modern. I have security of a kind, but not all I want. The world is full of men, my dear—men quite willing to oblige given the chance. But it so happens I'm fond of you—very *very* fond; the irony is it doesn't reach that far, if you get my meaning. To be your mistress might be an invigorating experience. But chancy. And I don't take chances. Why should I? I'm rich. I don't have to.'

'No.' He paused, wondering for a moment whether to play her along further, taunt her to some show of temper, then wisely refrained. Instead he asked, professing an uncharacteristic air of bewilderment, 'What *do* you want, Poppy?'

Poppy fetched a cigarette from a case on the mantelshelf, lit it, and after a few nervous puffs took the bull by the horns and said outwardly cool, 'It's what *you* want, isn't it? Me, or freedom.'

'You mean to have the knot securely tied?'

'Yes. That's it exactly.'

A drawn-out pause followed, in which her heart thudded so heavily she thought he must surely hear it. There was no other sound in her ears but the droning of a bee against the window. Just for a few moments she was acutely afraid. Then she heard Lloyd saying in curiously practical tones:

'All right. Marriage. Be my wife, Poppy, and I'll do my best providing you play your part. No frigid little girl airs; no wielding the purse strings. Share and share alike. Yes?'

She flung herself at him. 'Oh, Lloyd, you ridiculous creature. Of *course*. I'm not a *girl*—I don't flatter myself you haven't an eye on the main chance. All the same—'

The words were stifled on her lips as his mouth came down on hers. There was a rocking motion, and the chair toppled over, throwing them both on the floor. At the same moment any remaining glimmer of sunlight dimmed suddenly. A waft of cold air shivered the room as a shadow passed, followed by a high pitched scream that could have been that of an animal or a child from outside. Lloyd helped Poppy to her feet. She was shaking.

'What was that? Lloyd, did you hear?'

'Nothing,' he answered. 'One of those damned gulls, I expect.' But a trickle of sweat coursed down his forehead. As soon as possible, he thought, when things were formally settled between Poppy and himself, they'd get out of this place. There was something not quite right about the locality, something, for all his experience, he couldn't fathom.

From further up the lane the sound of music crept weirdly through the summer night.

Manfred Hearne's concerto.

*   *   *

The news of Poppy's and Lloyd's forthcoming marriage caused no great surprise round Summerhayes, though Adam commented to his wife that Walsh was on to a good thing.

'Maybe,' Lucinda said airily, 'except I bet he'll be disappointed. Poppy's a shrewd one and she has the cash. If you ask me she'll have him on a lead all right.'

'I doubt it,' Adam remarked drily. 'Lloyd's

no fool; he'll see everything's nicely tied up, financially, and Poppy will be wondering what the hell got into her.'

'Perhaps they'll have children,' Lucinda said musingly. 'You never know, Poppy's at the funny age—the menopause. It happens sometimes.'

'A youngster about would make a difference,' Adam said, with a condemning glance. 'That's one thing here that's wrong. Not a child among the whole bunch of us.'

'What do you expect from the Yvonne Court type?'

'Yvonne's not the only woman around,' Adam said meaningfully.

Lucinda wheeled round on him. 'Look, Adam, we did say *one* day,' she pointed out. 'But not yet. Not here.'

'Why not?'

'It's not suitable.'

'We can find somewhere else.'

Her lips tightened. 'I don't want to leave.'

'Of course not. Because of that bastard, Hearne.'

'Jealous?' she mocked.

Before he could answer there was a quiver of light that darkened almost immediately to dying, deepening grey; then it was gone.

Lucinda looked puzzled. 'Did you see that?'

'What?'

'I don't know,' she admitted. 'A sort of shadowiness. Odd.'

'Clouds coming up, I expect,' Adam said uncomfortably. 'They *do* sometimes, you know, even in summer.'

She went to the window and looked out. The sun was still comparatively high in a brilliant blue sky. No trace of a cloud, not even a feathered film of one anywhere.

'Nothing,' she remarked.

'What do you mean, nothing?'

'No cloud, no mist, no one about. Rather weird really.'

She looked so confused—almost afraid—he took her into his arms, pressing her head against his chest, his hand lingering momentarily against the rich softness of her hair. 'Idiot,' he murmured. He could feel her body relax into a sigh. As he released her, she said slowly, 'Perhaps you're right about us leaving. Perhaps we ought to go. But—'

'Yes?'

'What about Aleyne?'

He turned away abruptly. 'Aleyne has her own flat. She can go there or stay on here. That's up to her. She's not *our* affair.'

Lucinda laughed wryly. 'Oh, Adam, what a liar you are. Do you think I don't realise? Do you imagine for one moment even the *question* of Manfred would've come up if I hadn't known you were cursing yourself for throwing her over?'

'I didn't throw her over,' he said acidly. 'The business was mutual.'

'No, it wasn't. I fell for you, and that was that. We were all in it, all three. And we still are, darling. It'll work itself out, I suppose. So maybe we'd better not suggest leaving here again, either of us. I don't think it would be any good. We're sort of caught in an emotional vortex that's gone too far to get away from. I think it's the same with the rest of us. Yvonne, Poppy and Lloyd, the Carsons—even the Saunders. I mean, I think that *is* rather odd— such an ordinary down-to-earth pair. But maybe—' her voice faltered before she continued, 'maybe *that's* the answer.'

'What, for Pete's sake?'

'The earth,' Lucinda answered. 'It *could* be, couldn't it? Kind of haunted hungry ground, reaching out like a great spider to keep us here?'

She giggled nervously. But Adam did not smile. He was thinking, with surprise, that for Lucinda her statement had been quite profound. It had occurred to him more than once the surrounding terrain was in some curious way unique, as though the pocket of ground enclosing the few houses differed from the rest of the Cornish scene in some deeply significant way. It could be quiet and windless there, when a mile or so away high winds raged. Even when rain fell it held a more monotonous intensity, reminding him of the incessant beat of native drums from some faraway jungle.

He could not determine whether Manfred was at the root of it, with his fanatical dedication to Mag-Mell and Tir-Na-Noc, or merely, like the rest of their little crowd, a receptacle for unseen elemental forces. The problem, though disturbing, was also titivating to his writer's mind and when, later, he thought things over once more on his own, he quite discarded the idea of flight. His instinctive dislike of Hearne had increased rather than diminished, but so long as he kept his hands off Lucinda he'd play up in the cause of research—psychic or otherwise.

And Aleyne too, naturally.

If the fellow so much as touched one hair of her beautiful body, he'd take his great neck between his hands and squeeze the life out of him.

He caught himself up abruptly, shocked by his own violence. Good God! he thought, were we all potential murderers beneath the civilised facade?

He was so shaken that, when a few minutes later Aleyne came into the lounge, he hardly noticed her, was aware only of a slight shape in a blue-green flimsy long dress passing wraith-like, with a bowl of flowers to the table. When he came to his senses she was gone. He did not see her, with her fawn-silk hair about her shoulders walking leisurely towards Hearne's cottage; so the expression in her eyes, dream-like, entranced, escaped him. Neither did he catch the sighing sounds of Manfred's tune reverberating through the trees until minutes had passed. And then, abruptly, it ceased.

The wailing chords died only a minute before Aleyne reached Hearne's gate. He was standing on the path professing to examine a rose bush. At her approach he turned, smiling blandly.

'My dear girl, what a pleasant surprise,' he said. 'Here—what do you think of this?' He snapped off a half-open bloom, and strolled to meet her. 'A good specimen, isn't it?—Smell it.'

She took the flower mechanically, with life slowly returning to the blankness of her eyes. Like some puppet jerked by unseen strings she lifted it to her nostrils. The perfume nostalgically sweet and heady seemed to fill the air.

'Very,' she said mechanically, almost in a whisper.

'Won't you come in?'

Though something about him impelled her, she was reluctant. The words of an old rhyme floated from the far past through her brain—'Won't you walk into my parlour, said the spider to the fly?'—she closed her eyes briefly, steadying herself by clutching a gatepost. Then she said with a sudden revulsion of feeling, 'No thank you.'

'But, Aleyne, I *want* you to.'

Through the miasma of confusion she

jerked herself round and had already taken a step back when his hand fell on her shoulder forcing her to face him. His brilliant dark eyes became flames over her own. The sensuous mouth above the cleft chin was desirous, flooding her with response that at the same time was positively hateful. She jerked her head away abruptly. The rose dropped from her hand leaving a stain of blood on her palm from a thrusting thorn.

'Leave me alone,' she whispered. 'Don't ever touch me again.'

She could hear him laughing softly, mockingly, as she hurried from the path. Something lean and dark sprang before her from an overhanging tree, and stood spitting, green eyes blazing in feline hatred.

'Away you—' she found the courage to say, waving her arm threateningly. The creature arched its back and a moment later had sprung into the shadows. When she turned for a hasty glance behind her there was nothing there but the slim form of the boy Bran watching her with curious intentness by the hedge. He had a thorn stick in his hand, and was barefoot, looking like some malicious urchin from the wilds of nowhere. Despite this, Aleyne was aware of an intuitive perception about him strangely at variance with his youth. She was suddenly frightened; frightened of the unknown, and because nothing seemed to be quite what it purported to be. Of her own weakness also. Why had she allowed herself to be drawn to Manfred's at all? She didn't like him. She already sensed something evil lurking beneath his large exterior which transgressed far further than mere physical desire. Perhaps she should tell Adam. Perhaps she should leave, even if he and Lucinda didn't.

But when she reached the house she knew she wouldn't because so far she'd no proof of anything being amiss. Manfred had a perfect right to make a pass at her if she wandered alone so deliberately in his direction. She had only herself to blame. And except for a hand on her shoulder he hadn't even touched her. No—there was no point in making an issue of the incident; Adam would despise her, and Lucinda would laugh.

But that tune! And that wretched wild-looking boy! She suddenly felt icy cold. The trees were whispering, and a chill wind shivering up through the grass. Clouds were rising beyond the huddled wood. A harsh scream like the cry of some wild and hungry bird echoed balefully through the air. She hurried into the house and saw Adam on the way to his study with a thick book under his arm.

Lucinda came out of the lounge to meet her.

'Where've you been?' she asked curiously.

'For a stroll, I felt stuffy.'

'Well you look done up, rather a mess, I must say.'

Catching a glimpse of herself through the hall mirror, Aleyne had to agree. Large dark-rimmed eyes, untidy hair loose and straggling over her forehead, and not a tint of colour anywhere. Even her lips were pale.

'Yes, I feel it.'

Lucinda shrugged. 'You shouldn't go wandering. You've told *me* not to enough times. But then perhaps—' her voice faltered suggestively.

'Yes?'

'Perhaps you're trying to catch Manfred for yourself, is that it?'

Aleyne wheeled on her furiously. 'How can you suggest such a thing? He's—he's detestable—'

'I know, but fascinating. Even Adam knows it. He thinks there's something odd going on round here. Not only Beltane and the funny games. Something—unspeakable.'

'What do you mean?'

'I don't know. But Adam's going to find out, or at least try. He's gone to the study to look up some old encyclopaedia or other to find if there's a clue there; if not he's sending for a book from the library. You see, he's a hunch the land's wrong round here.'

'How?'

Lucinda shrugged again. 'Hard to say. You know Adam; he won't commit himself on just theories. And of course to admit the word "haunted" isn't his way at all. Everything in that category according to his male approach, must have a logical reason. He won't even accept Manfred's in any way out of the ordinary. But we know better, don't we?'

'Do we?'

'Oh come off it, Aleyne. You're as besotted as I am. When he plays the fiddle—or piano rather—we dance to his tune. Another thing—I've watched your eyes when he's near—'

'Be quiet,' Aleyne snapped, struggling with her anger.

Lucinda gave an edgy laugh.

'That's O.K. He's not *my* idea of a shining knight in armour either. But don't tell me any woman worth her salt doesn't have a secret passion for such overpowering male brutality. Can you imagine him as a lover?' A dreamy note crept into her voice. 'I can. And maybe that's the haunting around Summerhayes—something so earthy and strong there's no escape. Not in the end.' She broke off and turned away, continuing after a short pause, 'I've thought several times lately we should all three of us pack up and go away, because I'm not just a heartless bitch, you know. I *am* fond of Adam, and you, though you may find it hard to believe! We shan't go, though. Not only because you and I don't actually want to but because Adam's enmeshed himself. He's got his nose to the ground like a bloodhound now, and he won't give up until everything's solved. By then I'm afraid—'

'Yes?'

'It may be too late,' Lucinda concluded. 'And don't ask me what I mean, because I just couldn't tell you.'

Aleyne didn't reply, just stood watching Lucinda go upstairs slowly. Then she, too, jerked herself to movement, and went into the lounge.

The light was dying, sending quivering silvered rays across the carpet, catching Aleyne's strained profile into transient clarity. No abnormal shadow massed the pleasant interior, but a dreaded unacknowledged fear seemed to fill the atmosphere with taunting malicious unease. Aleyne went to the window, half expecting to hear the chords of a piano from the distance. But no sound came and presently she too went up to her room, trying hard to erase the brief conversation from her mind.

CHAPTER FIVE

Before making his intended trip to the large library at Penjust ten miles along the north coast, Adam paid a visit to the rectory at Magswikk in the hope of obtaining a few historical details concerning the vicinity of Summerhayes.

The rector, a bachelor, was a man probably

in his early sixties, small, squat, with a broad bland face, and genial smile that belied the disapproving wary glint of his narrow eyes.

'I would help you if I could,' he said when they were both seated in his large gloomy lounge. 'But a man of my calling steers away from harmful superstitions whenever possible. There are always stories put about in country districts. But—' he broke off pausing a moment, in which Adam sensed an intense observance that was disquietening.

'Yes?' he prompted.

'I was merely wondering why you were so concerned,' the flat voice continued expressionlessly. The lids were half-fallen over the small eyes again. Two stubby hands lay flat on the plump thighs. Adam could not help noticing how broad they were with wide, flattened finger tips.

'We haven't lived in the district long,' Adam answered. 'As newcomers we're naturally interested in the background.'

'We?'

'Our little group of residents round Summerhayes. Myself especially, of course, because I'm a writer.'

'Ah.' The sound rose and died in the stuffiness of the room like that of air escaping from a pricked balloon.

Adam waited, and when nothing more was forthcoming added. 'We haven't had much cooperation from the natives—Magswikk I

66

mean. I've even fancied sometimes that we're resented.'

The portly figure got up, moved to an archaic-looking mahogany sideboard, and returned with two glasses and a decanter on a tray.

'Will you have a little fortifier, sir? Just to prove sociability still exists here?'

Adam agreed reluctantly. The whisky was good, and some of his tension eased.

'You mentioned the word resentment,' the rector continued when he was seated again. 'Well, there may be a little, among the inhabitants. Until the land was broken up and those new places built, it was considered almost as common ground. There was a right of way through the wood—a short cut to the coast—which is now blocked by someone's garden. You can't expect Cornish people to appreciate that kind of plunder—'

'Plunder? Oh, but really! Hardly that.'

'Why not? What else is it when strangers—foreigners—come from up-country and grab without a by-your-leave large plots of our own land?'

'The ground was properly purchased and paid for,' Adam pointed out. 'Most of it belonged to the estate of the late Sir Bradley Carven—'

The bullet head shook vigorously and Adam noticed with distaste how the plump pale jowls wobbled. The voice was aggressive when his

67

companion said, 'You can't *buy* land, sir—not *that* kind. It belongs to itself; except—for those whose mortal and immortal remains lie there.'

Just for a second, one hand traced a faint gesture of a cross on the air, though Adam just then could not accept any spiritual significance—he was aware only of a deepening sense of desecration and repugnance.

'Well,' he said getting up abruptly, 'I'm sorry to have troubled you. Obviously you've no useful information to give me. I ought to have thumbed the libraries first. There must be historical records. Excuse me for bothering you. Good afternoon.'

He walked sharply out towards the hall door, but the tubby figure with incredible soft-footed speed, was there before him.

'Allow me,' he said opening it, 'and good day to you.'

Adam strode down the narrow garden path with the uncomfortable impression that the unprepossessing character was still watching him from the porch. At the gate he glanced back, and saw the door closing slowly, as though through its own volition. The sky was darkening subtly. Everything had a grey dejected appearance—even the thin wind-blown trees, round the granite house, which were already yellowing, and shedding leaves, though it was still high summer. On the opposite side of the lane the old church stood grey and sombre in its patch of looming grave-stones. The general aspect was of neglect. Sparse weeds and a few twisted thorns and rose trees straggled among forgotten monuments, many of which were leaning at an angle, as though tired of having stood erect for so many centuries. The building and the rectory were on a raised hillock overlooking the village beneath, and as he cut down to the shop for cigarettes, Adam wondered how long it was since anyone had been buried there. There was probably a newer cemetery somewhere in the vicinity he thought, then forced his thoughts away with an effort, from such an unsavoury subject.

Mrs Trewartha was as uncommunicative as the rector when he made a tentative enquiry concerning Summerhayes.

'Oh,' she said, 'I don't go in for history or delving into such things. That land round there's seen many a queer going on, I don't doubt. But folks who's bred an' born here knows better than to go pokin' into what don't concern them. And I advise you to do the same, surr—just leave things alone, and then maybe in time people will accept you for what you are.'

'And that is?'

Her heady eyes flickered with a tinge of humour. 'Furriners, Mr Vance, Surr, but harmless and good for trade now an' again. I can't say fairer than that, can I?'

'No,' Adam agreed. 'I suppose not. Thank you.'

He walked back to the house with the frustrated feeling of having come to a dead end; and yet he was convinced that something of significance lay behind the rector's ambiguity and Eliza's putting off tactics, and decided to go to Penjust the following day for a thorough search through the library.

There must be records of some kind dealing with land survey and a history—however trivial—of details of past events in the Magswikk area. Even a legend might have a grain of truth—some clue to follow up that would prove a valuable lead.

So he set off early in the car, and arrived at Penjust by ten-thirty. The town, approached from a straggling main road of cottages for tin workers at the mines, consisted of a large square from which three streets led off to shops, a church and a seventeenth century pub. A pleasant surprise, Adam thought, after its rather depressing outskirts; the library certainly looked promising, having recently been modernised and partially rebuilt. He was told at the desk of the fiction department that if he wished to give his name and address he could have a borrower's ticket. 'But that doesn't mean the reference section,' she said. 'No books can go out from there. You can *look* of course, anyone's free to do that.'

Adam was mildly amused. Despite her

70

owlish glasses, and air of authority, she was obviously very young, with smooth plumpish cheeks and long fair hair falling over her shoulders.

'I shall be glad to have a ticket,' he told her, 'thank you. But first of all if you tell me where the reference section is, I'll have a dig round. History. I'm looking for a book on—the occult.'

Her reaction to the last word was unhelpful.

'Oh I don't know if we've got *that*. Ghosts, you mean? Hauntings?'

'Not exactly. But anything of the kind would help.'

'Well—you should go upstairs then, and into the room on the left. The books are in alphabetical order, and marked above. I'm afraid I can't help more.'

Adam thanked her, and made his way to the reference section. It was a large department lined on all four sides by books and he was surprised to see no librarian in charge. But he found the tabulation excellent, and after half an hour's browsing discovered an ancient volume titled *Local Legends. Truth and Facts*.

He took it to the window, studied the index and found Magswikk listed there, with a sub title 'Witches and Demons'.

The paragraph was brief, stating merely that three witches, Margaret Kyrle, her sister Deborah and niece Mercy, were hanged in 1698 near Magswikk on the edge of a wood, for dealing in malpractice. The elder Margaret Kyrle, commonly known as Black Mag, from which the village got its present name, was said to own a cat called Satan who could assume any shape at will, either human or of a toad, and killed man or beast when it felt inclined. The spot of execution was now marked by three very ancient twisted elder trees growing on the fringe of the wood. Legend had it that the three trees housed the spirits of the witches and were indestructible. They had been cut down from time to time, but after a period always appeared again. Even lightning had failed to eradicate their growth. The main witness at the trial of the unfortunate women was said to have been an unsavoury priest of the parish, Silas Carnverrych, who was himself of doubtful reputation, and reputed to have made advances to the girl Mercy, who repulsed him.

Glancing at the date of the volume, Adam saw that it had been published in 1810 in only a limited edition.

He put the book back thoughtfully, and in a mood of pre-occupation went downstairs to find the girl at the desk had been joined by a pale scholarly looking young man obviously of senior position there, who appeared anxious to impress.

'I hope you found what you wanted, sir?' He said politely. 'My assistant was telling me you were making enquiries concerning the occult.

If there's any particular book you need that we haven't got here, I can probably obtain it for you.'

'Thank you very much,' Adam answered. 'I was lucky enough to find what I needed.' He paused before adding, 'You've an excellent selection of books. I shall always know where to come when I'm needing information.'

He spent a few more minutes over the necessary formalities of getting a borrower's ticket, then left. The sky had clouded during his interval at the library, and as the car turned from the main street into the moorland road leading to Summerhayes the bleakness of the landscape struck him with new intensity—wild moors above ragged hedgerows topped by granite boulders or standing stones. Here and there the stark ruins of ancient mine-stacks were outlined like skeletons against the hills and horizon. Ditches on either side of the lane were riotous with ferns, bluebells and foxgloves. Gorse flamed in patches between heather and strewn boulders on the slopes, but soon, he thought, with a queer sense of apprehension, blossom time would be over. The grim countryside would revert to its primeval character of wind-swept terrain and barren earth stretching in desolate rock-hewn folds to the sea—a reminder of far ancient times when man had first evolved to inhabit the scene of the earth's early eruption.

A wind had risen, bowing the sparse trees

towards the north, sending a scurry of flying leaves against the windscreen. Adam suddenly shivered, and drew his side-window up. Automatically he was reminded of the three witches said to be hanged on the fringe of the wood near Summerhayes. Was it possible that some lingering dark echo of previous events still lingered? He wasn't normally the superstitious type. But as he drove along he became increasingly and uncomfortably aware of many small unsavoury incidents that hadn't properly registered in his mind before. His life with Lucinda for instance, their too-frequent bickerings and mutual distrust overshadowed by his own compelling instincts for violence and assertion of male superiority. The affair of Beltane, for example, when any feeling he had for her had become briefly one of mere brutality. And his jealousy of Aleyne. The shadowed moments in which his brain had become a malevolent receptacle for revenge against Manfred Hearne. Revenge? For what? As far as he knew Manfred had done none of them any actual harm, except in thought. Yes. But thought was strong. The reactions of all of them at that ridiculous celebration in the woods had proved that concentrated will-power from even one individual as solely dedicated as Hearne, could itself be an entity and potential destroyer.

And when winter came, if they were still there, there was the prospect of Samain ahead.

Manfred half-banteringly had already issued a challenge that the little crowd should be present with him to celebrate the dread feast of ancient Celtic times—

'A game, if you take it as such,' he'd said, with a glint in his eyes of ironic amusement, 'but a very potent one I can assure you; of course no one who is afraid should attend. Fear itself can kill, which would be of immense satisfaction to Crom Cruaich. On the other hand—to the brave comes great victory and the full satisfaction of partaking in the vast companionship of Mag-Mell itself—'

This announcement had taken place on the last social gathering only a fortnight ago, at the Saunders' house; Manfred, uninvited for once, had arrived late. But lateness had not, apparently, diminished his prowess at dominating either the atmosphere or conversation. Adam remembered uncomfortably Yvonne's starry gaze upon him, and her hushed question of 'Oh, Manfred, do explain. About Crom Cruaich, I mean—what is he? Who?'

Adam had tried to divert attention with a certain amount of light-hearted sarcasm. But the drift of the answer had penetrated distastefully—allusions to the Dark God, sacrifices, ordeals by fire and water, of spiritual darkness in which human beings were likely to be attacked by evil supernatural powers.

'We though, as initiated individuals, are

capable of withstanding any hostile force,' Hearne had finally commented. 'As I said, it is a challenge for any who feel sufficiently fortified to face it.'

'The cunning bastard,' Adam had thought then. 'A fraud. No more.'

Now driving along the deserted lane under the lowering, still darkening sky, he wondered. The very atmosphere and view had become menacing. Even the distant sea had an inky sombre quality beyond the rim of cliffs, a startling clarity which was intensified, heralding, he guessed, the threat of rain. But it was not until he approached the wood that the shadow descended; a sudden clawing blackness before his eyes. He braked involuntarily, lifting one hand to his face. A moment later when he looked up, all was normal, except for a faint quiver of the landscape that instantaneously faded.

A little shaken he started up again, and by the time he reached the house had almost convinced himself there had been nothing unusual about the unpleasant incident. It had merely been a trick of light; or perhaps his eyes were wrong. He would have to get them tested.

But it was not his eyes. Neither was a perfectly ordinary trick of light responsible. Though nobody about Summerhayes admitted it, each in turn was aware of the sinister undercurrents and significant apparitions which though formless were the more frightening because of it. Secrecy under a veneer of brittle social communication, insidiously spread from one to another. Even Lloyd and Poppy were reluctant to air their own childish notions.

Aleyne became moody and abstracted, fearing yet longing for the nameless thing she could not define. Lucinda, with earthy self-awareness, was obsessed inwardly with Manfred despite occasional sneering comments calculated to deceive Adam.

But he was not deceived for a moment. If he could he was determined to save her from herself, more for her own good than his. Her physical exuberance and potential lasciviousness now not only jarred but revolted him. How ironic, he thought frequently, that a group of socialites in search of Manfred's legendary Mag-Mell and 'eternal youth' could become in such a short time so painfully macabre—uneasy caricatures of their former selves, with their inward faults magnified to ludicrous proportions like creatures in a puppet play.

One afternoon, soon after his visit to Penjust, he took a walk to the further side of the wood nearest to Magswikk. The trees there, from majestic beech, sturdy oak, and a few pines intermingled with larch, thinned out to twisted sloes and thorn, eventually becoming a patch of furze and scrubland. The earth had a dank smell, and was dark in places, as though deep in bog. But the ground seemed firm, and he walked on, while a mournful wind stirred the grasping branches of the trees, sending quivering shadows across the sparse yellowing grass.

An air of dejection and deep melancholy lay there.

His instinct was to hurry off, and retrace his way past Manfred's cottage back to Summerhayes; but he forced himself on, sensing that here, if anywhere, he must find what he'd come to look for.

A minute or so later he knew he was right. Immediately round a bend in the land, grotesquely silhouetted on a raised hummock against the paper-pale sky, were the stark dark shapes of three grotesquely twisted trees—elders from the look of them, but leafless, with blackened trunks and crippled arms of branches clawing outwards and down as though in supplication or cursing in the face of death. He took a step forward, feeling his own nerves tauten as a gust of air sent their skeleton shadows quivering to his feet. No leaf fluttered. There was no sound at all but the sighing wind through the undergrowth interspersed with a creaking of ancient wood.

He was aware of a creeping intensifying sense of evil emanating from the very ground where he stood, and then, suddenly, as he turned, forcing himself sharply back the way he'd come, he heard a shrill high-pitched scream that could have been of a maniac, or more logically perhaps, a bird's frightened cry.

Insisting to himself it must be the latter, he quickened his pace, and was almost running when he approached Hearne's cottage.

Just before he got there he saw a lean young shape standing near the trees at the side of the path. He had an air of amusement about him. His bright eyes flickered with an alien teasing light. In the fading glow of the misted sun, his black curls were tipped with gold which gave momentarily the impression of crested horns.

Bran.

'Blast the boy,' Adam thought, giving a curt nod as he passed. The whole thing had been contrived by him as a trick to frighten. He looked back once, but the youth, child, or whatever he could be called, had gone. In his place was a static feline shape with arched back, and narrowed gleaming emerald eyes, watching malignantly it seemed, from the shadows.

The confrontation could have lasted only seconds. Then, with lightning speed the shape sprang and was taken into the clustered darkness of the trees. Adam walked on, annoyed not only by events, but at himself for having been so unnerved.

When he reached Summerhayes he found Lucinda restlessly pacing the lounge.

'Where've you been?' she demanded with the new edge to her voice that was becoming familiar these days. She was looking flushed and untidy, with a sullen curl to her mouth that made him want to slap her.

'Does it matter?' his voice was curt. 'Merely a stroll round. Why? What's the matter with you?'

'Nothing,' she answered, 'except that it can be lonely here. Sometimes I get edgy; depressed I suppose.'

'Where's Aleyne?'

She shrugged. 'God knows. With Manfred perhaps. I don't know.'

He took her by both shoulders, shaking her briefly far more violently than he'd intended. 'What do you mean—with Manfred? If—'

Lucinda gaped at him. 'For Heaven's sake, Adam. Is she that important to you? You must be crazy. Anyway—I didn't mean it.'

He let her go, and turned, ashamed for his lapse, head in his hands. 'Sorry,' he muttered, facing her again. 'I didn't mean to do that. But when you mentioned Hearne—'

'Oh I know. You don't like him. No need to apologise. But for goodness' sake, Adam, get this thing you have about Aleyne and Manfred out of your head. I can assure you you've no need to worry. Our Mr Hearne has other fish to fry.'

'What do you mean?'

Lucinda gave a wry gesture of contempt and amusement. 'Our so-nice Miss Court. Yvonne. *She's* there, darling, undergoing the great seduction act probably.'

'How do you know?'

'My dear Adam, I watched her. All diaphanous and coy in a see-through drapery thing when she set off. Having nothing to do I followed—unnoticed of course. But he was in the garden, and ushered her inside just as though he was expecting her. Actually it's been going on for quite some time now. Didn't you know?'

Adam didn't reply.

'No. I suppose not. Men aren't always so quick on the uptake over these things. What I can't fathom for the life of me, though, is what he sees in her. I mean to say—Miss *Court* in bed. Really rather funny when you think about it.'

But Lucinda's voice held no amusement; only, Adam decided, a bitter pang of jealousy which was far too acute for her to hide.

He knew then, that far the wisest course would be for them to pack up and take off, especially with autumn and Samain following. At the same time he was lethargically aware that they wouldn't, and that however much he tried, Lucinda, when it came to the point, would refuse.

So he let matters drift.

They all did.

And when October came they were still there uneasily waiting for the unknown that was to come.

81

CHAPTER SIX

In October the weather was still comparatively mild, though morning and evening mists crept milky-white over the landscape, taking moors and woods into a quivering grey uniformity. That period of the year was usually stimulating for Adam's writing. But this time it didn't happen. Though he determinedly shut himself in his study for certain hours each day, usually the mornings—his mind, rather than his brain, wouldn't function in the right direction. The format of his new play was in order, the characters clearly defined. But when it came to action a curious deadness descended on them, making their behaviour seem contrived, and to him artificial.

He would sit for periods at his desk with paper before him in the typewriter, blank and meaningless; it occurred to him frequently that instead of bringing peace and the impetus to work, Summerhayes was draining any decent ambition from him. Yet he seemed incapable of taking the necessary steps to get away. Sometimes he thought with sudden irrational longing, of Aleyne. On many occasions he had paused outside her room, fighting the impulse to go in and make love to her, with or without her permission. But always in the end he went on after a few moments, knowing this was not the way he wanted things. Though unconventional in many respects, and with a rational view of sex, which was in itself to his male mind as much a necessity as eating and breathing, Aleyne came into a different category altogether. He had realised for a long time what a fool he'd been in giving her up. But the deed was done. Unless she came back to him of her own free will ready to face the issue squarely, enabling them to go ahead together, he wanted none of her—no furtive half-measures or sexy interludes. Her mind as much as her body mattered. With Aleyne he would have been happily monogamous. Whereas Lucinda! At such a point he'd break off any attempt to write, get up sharply, with a sensual desire—almost compulsion, stirring him to action.

If his wife was around, and the moment propitious, he'd drown his finer instincts in her very gorgeous and available body, feeling a sense of shame or conscience when she protested eventually, 'Oh, Adam—haven't you had enough? For God's sake—' she'd pull herself free then, while he'd note with bitter pleasure the luscious body still pulsing from his ravishing.

Oh yes; Lucinda was a tasty possession. But he knew, from her glance, frequently, that she was aware of being little more than that.

Once she said coldly, with a touch of

contempt as she dressed herself, 'You don't care a damn for me really, do you, Adam? You've a nasty habit of making me feel like a whore sometimes.'

Contrition filled him. He noted for the first time the shadowed, almost hurt look of her eyes, the quiver of dropping lips. Was that what he was doing to her then? Offering degradation instead of love to the woman he'd married? For a time after that incident he was considerate to her, under a simulation of tenderness, thrusting Aleyne to the back of his mind.

With Lucinda it was different.

She did not forget, but kept the memory alive, finding in it justification for her obsession with Manfred.

*　　*　　*

Lucinda told herself it was *fate* when she lost her scarf one day over Manfred's gate. A wind was billowing, and in a mood of desperation to be away from the house where a tense atmosphere was knife-sharp between Aleyne and Adam, she plunged out into the grey afternoon wearing a Swedish anorak, with a scarlet square over her head. Instinctively she took the path towards Hearne's. A little earlier she'd detected a few wailing chords from his piano, rising and falling in the restless soughing and swish of trees and undergrowth.

When she was half way there the sound had stopped. But the impulse of her senses had electrified. In a sudden abandonment of frustration she tore the silk thing from her head, leaving the burnished hair wild and streaming from her face. The next moment it had been whipped from her hand, and she watched it momentarily caught on a freak gust and taken away like an inflated miniature balloon until it descended rapidly to land on a may tree inside Manfred's garden.

She paused, with her heart quickening. She couldn't possibly reach the silly looking bit of material, which really did appear rather ridiculous, like an illustration she'd seen in a picture book as a child, of an old crow wrapped up in a red handkerchief. It meant nothing to her. She had numerous scarves and squares tucked away in a drawer at the house. Still, she told herself reasoningly and as an excuse for retrieving it, Adam had given it to her. He might be hurt if she just left it to rot away on a thorny branch in Manfred Hearne's garden.

Adam—*hurt*? The idea was quite monstrous really. He wouldn't care two pins—no more than he did for *her*, which was another legitimate reason for doing what she did.

As she walked up the path to the front porch she knew a compulsion stronger than any emotion she had ever felt before—a desire so overwhelming for Manfred's presence it seemed that all the strain and inhibitions of the past weeks and months had been brought to their final conclusive culmination—a point of no return when they could face each other with the barriers down. A touch of his hand, his whisper of her name against her cheek, a sigh, a murmur, and softening of his mouth which she kissed a hundred times in her dreams— 'Oh Manfred, Manfred—' her heart and senses cried—'I'm here, waiting. I've waited so long. Want me, please want me'—nothing else mattered but that; to be desired and taken by the dark earthy force of the one man who could bring peace and forgetfulness. And afterwards? There was no afterwards; only the deep primitive sense of present awareness that had its roots long long ago when the earth was new and man first gazed on woman.

At the door she paused, bemused and still, though the air was fresh and chill with a driving spatter of rain in it. There was no sound from inside. She did not even hear the firm tread of footsteps down the hall before the latch was unfastened and he stood silhouetted in the uncertain light, waiting for her to speak. When she did not, he said quietly, 'So you've come.' There was a short laugh. 'I thought you would—one day.'

'Didn't you want me to?' Her voice was a whisper in her own ears. She had forgotten the scarf, the casual apology she'd intended to make; the false facade.

'Of course,' he said, 'in your own good time.'

He paused before adding, 'And mine.'

'I didn't mean to—I hope it's convenient—you see—' she broke off, shaking, realising the futility of words.

He put his hand on her shoulder. 'Come along. It's cold.'

She shivered, but her cheeks and body were on fire. He led her by the hand upstairs, and she was aware of a tremendous rush of passion as he disrobed her first, savouring slowly each curve of her glowing body, then lay her firmly but gently on the bed. She didn't see the secret sly look of triumph on his face as he bore down on her, or hear from outside the wind's sudden rising to a high pitch of laughter. All she knew was a flood of such wild fulfilment the room around her was lost and dark—a whirling vortex of appeasement that left her temporarily weak and unaware of the world.

She opened her eyes presently.

'Manfred,' she said softly raising her arms. 'Oh, Manfred—I love you—'

'*Love*?' he echoed, and his voice was strident, merciless. 'Get up and put your clothes on. You look a fool lying there.'

He sauntered to the mirror, adjusted his trousers and shirt and surveyed his reflection complacently. A handsome face. But suddenly—*vile*, Lucinda thought hysterically.

She sprang from the bed, and clutched her underwear frantically. 'You beast—' she said through her teeth, 'to say *that*. After—after—'

'It was what you wanted, wasn't it? Well, you've had it.'

He turned, ambled back to her and took her chin in his hand. 'And remember my dear, to keep your mouth shut. But you will of course. In fact for your own sake you'll do just what I tell you to, and whenever I say so. Understood?'

By then her teeth were chattering. She didn't reply, merely dressed herself with frenzied haste, and a minute later was running down the lane towards Summerhayes.

*   *   *

Aleyne was in the hall arranging ferns and greenery in a bowl when her sister came through the door. Lucinda's appearance shocked her. 'What's the matter?' she asked. 'Has something happened? You look frightful.'

'I know what I look like. A fool. I've just been told.' Lucinda's eyes were wild in her white face, her mouth drawn with misery.

'But—'

'Stop it. It's none of your affair.' The distraught figure rushed past and up the stairs. Seconds later Aleyne heard the sharp snap of a door closing. She stood undecisively for a few moments wondering whether to follow, and then decided against it. Though she couldn't be certain she was pretty sure that Manfred Hearne was responsible for Lucinda's wild mood. Adam had gone to Penjust for books, and anyway she couldn't visualise him rousing such extreme reactions in her sister. He'd be ashamed in the first place. 'A fool'—Adam would never be that contemptuous—even if he felt it. And it wasn't true. In her own way Lucinda had her head pretty firmly screwed on.

Half an hour later there was a rap at the door. Aleyne went to open it and found Bran there, standing with Lucinda's red headscarf in his hand.

'For the lady,' he said, with a knowing half smile.

Lucinda appeared at the top of the stairs. As soon as she saw Bran she hurried down. 'Yes. It's mine. Where did you get it?'

His large luminous dark eyes opened wide with feigned innocence. 'From the tree. Where you left it.'

Lucinda snatched the material from his hand. 'I didn't leave it. It blew.'

The boy's smile widened. 'I know, I *know*.' He didn't turn immediately but waited, staring at her; and for a few moments his slender presence seemed to assume maturity. She saw him as he'd be perhaps in five, ten years' time, a proud unprincipled seducer of women, beautiful in the untamed way of wild creatures. A young monarch of the earthy world he inhabited.

The interim between them was brief, but

holding the timeless knowledge of the ages. Then Lucinda said shrilly with a wave of her hand, 'Go on, run away now. Thank you for the scarf.'

The smile died; his eyes narrowed before he turned and sped in his soft-footed way down the path into the lane. As his form disappeared the light faded perceptibly. Lucinda lifted her hand to her eyes, waiting for the shadow to disperse. She was shaking when she looked up. Aleyne was watching her. She too was pale.

'Did you notice anything?' Lucinda asked.

'I *felt* it,' Aleyne replied. 'Although I don't know what.'

'No.'

'Maybe we're getting neurotic,' Aleyne said after a pause. 'Shadows, and cats screaming, and silly boys trying to impress—' her voice faded uncertainly.

'No, but—that's *it*, isn't it?' Lucinda said, turning the red scarf nervously in her hands. '*Is* he a boy, *really*?'

'What do you mean?'

'I don't know, I really don't. Just for a moment—I know it was idiotic—but I was remembering what Hearne said, about Mag-Mell, and a minute being seven mortal years—'

Aleyne stimulated a laugh. 'I realise Manfred impresses you, Luce, but surely not *that* far—'

'*Manfred*?' Lucinda's voice rose shrilly. '*Impress*? What are you talking about? He's a

90

boor and a sadistic bully with the gift of the gab, that's all. I loathe him, do you understand? And that's true—really really *true*.' She caught Aleyne by the shoulders staring hard into her face. 'Do you believe me?'

'Yes, *now*,' Aleyne answered. 'You *think* you do anyway. So what he says isn't really important, is it?'

Lucinda's arms dropped flacidly to her sides.

'I'm not sure. That's a different thing altogether. Oh heavens!' her body suddenly relaxed. 'What about a drink? I really am all in, and that's a fact.'

'A good idea,' Aleyne agreed.

As they went into the lounge, a dark lean form sprang past the window, followed by a shriek holding the high crescendo of broken laughter.

Aleyne's hand trembled as she put the decanter on the table. 'That beastly cat,' she said. 'I've never wanted to strangle anything in my life before. But at the moment I'd gladly do it.'

'Oh, no, you wouldn't,' Lucinda told her, 'you'd never catch it in the first place. And if you did—well you were always the soft-hearted kind. Neither of us are born murderers, Ally. Just a couple of muddling frightened women in an emotional mess.'

Aleyne knew her sister was right there.

91

What she *didn't* know was that from then onwards it was not Manfred Lucinda dreamed about, but Bran.

CHAPTER SEVEN

'Hiram,' Rose said one day towards the end of October, 'I think we should say something, or get out.'

Her husband took his pipe out of his mouth—he still stuck to his pipe though cigars would have been more in keeping with his pocket—and waited for a moment staring reflectively at his wife's homely reflection with concern in his blue eyes. 'Tell them? What do you mean, love?'

She frowned and answered a little sharply for her, 'Oh go on! Don't *pretend*, Hiram. You know very well. About him—Mr Hearne.'

'Hm. A queer character, that's true enough. But we don't *know* anything do we? There's not a thing wrong to pin on him—'

'I'm not so sure. This feast that's coming, Samain, we'll be expected to go, and I don't like such carryings on. Don't seem healthy to me.'

'We're not bound to turn up,' Hiram said stolidly. 'It's up to us.'

'*Is* it though?' Rose's voice was doubtful. 'I wonder.'

'Now Rose don't *you* go getting a bee in your bonnet,' Hiram said a trifle testily. 'There are enough of that sort around already. *More* than enough. But I don't see why we should let them push us out. I've spent a hell of a lot on this place, love, and I mean to get what enjoyment I can out of it for a bit. Money's all right if it's used properly, but I never aimed to be moving about here and there all the time. We've not been here a year yet, and a taste of country's good after that town place. Oh come on, Rose, what've you got to complain of—*actually*?'

For some moments Rose didn't reply, then she said, 'The atmosphere, Hiram, as I said; the carryings on. Everyone's very friendly to us, I'll not deny. But there's something underneath I can't explain; something phoney. I know I'm not the clever sort, but it seems to me there's not a single happy couple around. And it's mostly that man's fault. Hearne's.'

'Think so?'

'Of course. He reckons he can do what he likes with anyone he chooses, and everyone's changing. It isn't that I believe in magic or spells or those silly feasts of his, but look at Yvonne—poor Miss Court—she's an odd one these days, Hiram. Ever since the Beltane carry-on. That's when it started. Oh, I've got eyes in my head. Snooping off to Hearne's place at all hours—and Lucinda, Adam's wife. If you ask me there's a lot we don't know about going on there—'

'Well, it's their affair. You've always said folks' business was their own, and I guess that's what we should remember.'

'No, Hiram, *no*.' Rose's voice was unexpectedly firm. 'It's ours too. Now if you agree I'll get something going—a sort of Round-Robin. We'll call a meeting first and make a suggestion we all turn down any more feast affairs. Poppy and Lloyd to begin with; Poppy's bright enough to know what's what, and she could get on to the others—'

'No. Not them,' Hiram said firmly. 'Poppy's O.K. I like her. And as you know I get on with Walsh—but there's a funny side to him. A bit of an exhibitionist when he feels like it. If we've *got* to get the ball rolling—and I can see you've set your mind on it, try Adam. A normal sort of chap; and I've a hunch you're right; he *is* going through a bad time with that wife of his. Probably jump at the chance of getting a dig at Hearne. His sister-in-law's a nice girl too. Sometimes I reckon—'

'Yes, Hiram?'

'Nothing,' he answered abruptly. 'What I think's got nothing to do with it. You know how I feel about not interfering with other people's lives, and I still say it's best to let well alone—'

'But it's *not* well,' Rose interrupted. '*Nothing* is, round here. I feel like you about the place, dear—it's a lovely spot and to have a bit of peace is grand. I thought when we first came

94

how lucky we were. But things've changed. All this arty business, clever talk, and fancy notions of magic and going back into the past. Why—do you realise—it's the way *mad* folk carry on. And if we stay on here I'm not going to be a part of it, I tell you straight. So stand by me, Hiram, or I'll pack my bags and leave on my own if necessary.'

Hiram knew his wife well enough to realise that when she got that certain note in her voice and set to her mouth, she meant it. Rose could be led so far, but she had her limits, and at a certain point could be as stubborn as a mule.

'All right, all right, love,' he told her. 'I agree with you. You take a stroll round to Adam's and put your point. I'll attend any meeting you arrange, only don't expect me to run it. This is *your* baby, Rose, and if you put all your weight behind it I'll back you against Manfred any day.' He slapped her fondly. She grinned.

'Now you stop needling me about my weight, Hiram. It's better to be plump and sane than lean and demented like that pathetic Court woman.'

He planted a kiss on her pink cheek. 'You don't have to remind me. I know a good thing when I've got it.'

A little later Rose set off for Summerhayes.

There was no wind, but the air was cold with a mist rising in curdling grey coils from the damp earth. A few last leaves like drooping dead hands hung from the branches of chestnut trees and sycamores. Branches dripped from the moisture, and bushes and undergrowth rose claw-like draped with the glitter of spider's webs.

Humming a little tune, Rose strode sturdily on, her sensible brogues crackling twigs into the squelchy ground underfoot. Not the kind of day she'd normally choose for a walk, but the challenge of whipping Adam's enthusiasm to combined action stimulated her. At one point when her woollen headscarf caught on the jagged branch of a thorn tree, she thought she heard the strains of Manfred's piano from the distance.

That beastly tune.

She paused uncertainly, and at the same moment it died into silence. A bird flew close by across her face. She lifted her hand. 'Shoo—shoo—go away you.' There was a curious scream, more of a cackle really, with a sudden thickening of the mist which became a blanket of fog creeping into her eyes and nose, half choking her. She waited until it had cleared, then started off again with her heart beating heavily and unpleasantly against her ribs and ears. Almost simultaneously one foot stumbled over a stone. A branch tore at her collar, and she fell, twisting her ankle painfully.

She lay shocked for more than a minute, before managing, with the aid of a nearby stunted tree, to drag herself to her feet. Obviously she hadn't broken anything, which was a mercy. But it was equally obvious she could hardly make the rest of the walk to Adam's with any safety. Her ankle and foot ached badly, and the only sensible course was to get back somehow to her own home. So she started off, hobbling with difficulty, and the aid of a stick.

She didn't see the feline shape leap from the trees across the path behind her, or notice a pale, drawn face watching her from a cluster of black trunks. The visage was twisted into a smirk of malignant satisfaction, the thin form stooping and witch-like.

A little later, when Rose was out of sight, Yvonne Court emerged from the shadows and made her way to Hearne's cottage.

He was waiting for her.

'Well done,' he said as he opened the door. 'Congratulations, my good and faithful servant. Now you shall have your reward. A little manipulation, yes?'

Her eyes were wide with dog-like devotion as she gaped at him, murmuring, 'Yes, oh yes.'

She climbed automatically on to the couch in his sitting room, where he gently and insidiously undressed her. Then he turned her over. His hands were quiet and caressing on her thin body, titivating each quivering nerve to hungry life. What she waited for she didn't comprehend. But fulfilment was always withheld, leaving her a slave to the hunger that possessed her. She did not see the smile of contempt on his lascivious face, or realise one small part of the inner revulsion he felt for her sterility.

She was merely a thing to him. His slave, whereas he, to her, was the dark god that had become her only reason for living.

'Bran,' he called presently, 'show Miss Court out.'

The boy appeared, with a knowing look in his brilliant dark eyes, and at that moment he did not really look so young after all.

When the door had closed and Yvonne's figure was disappearing down the lane, Hearne, with an immense sigh of satisfaction, poured himself a drink. He settled himself into an armchair, and as though from nowhere his cat appeared, leaping with alacrity on to his lap. The emerald eyes were wildly bright with delight and exhilaration. Its purring filled the room.

'We're doing well, Sam,' Manfred said speculatively, stroking the satin smoothness of its triangular head. 'But we have more—much more to do. She's beautiful—that fair little madam, and in the end she'll be one of us. Aleyne—Aleyne—' his tongue moistened his lips as desire swelled up in him. Then abruptly he pushed the cat away and went to the piano.

With weird intimidating chill, the tune rose and fell through the autumn air. And in her room at Summerhayes Aleyne heard, stiffened, and went to the window. By then the mist had thickened into fog.

Evening was closing in early.

'Oh God,' she whispered. 'Help me. What am I to do?'

There was a disturbance and curdling of the fog as though a shape had passed, then nothing more.

Very slowly she turned and went downstairs.

*   *   *

The brush of cobwebs and cloying air were thick and clammy on her face as she made her way half blindly down the track—a white shadow in the milky whiteness of the encroaching mist. Occasionally the slap of a leaf or twig flapped her cheek. Her stance was rigid, arms extended before her as though in automatic welcome to a force that had become stronger than her own will or comprehension. Yet behind the glazed stare of her eyes intermittent moments of awareness whispered 'Go back—go back'—she'd pause then, struggling to drag her stiffened limbs to obey. But the urge would pass and she'd press ahead as the whining melody sighed and soughed through bushes and trees, gaining impetus until her whole being was suffused and submerged in it, and she became no more than a whispered echo of Manfred's desire.

It was at the bend of the lane that the face appeared. Long, white with huge sunken eyes above the distorted mouth. Just for a second Aleyne was shocked to full consciousness. She stopped, with her hand at her throat. A pair of pale quivering hands came towards her; words, holding more the hiss of a serpent than any human quality, shattered the tune's insidious spell.

'Go back, you bitch, the way you came. He's not for you. He's mine—mine—' the tones died into a spate of such foul language Aleyne felt the blood drain from her trembling body, then flood her nerves and muscles to sudden mobility.

She turned and ran; stumbling and rushing instinctively with her heart pounding against her ribs. When she reached Summerhayes Adam was already coming out to look for her.

'What on earth's the matter?' he demanded, pulling her to him. 'My God! tell me, Aleyne— if that devil—it's Manfred isn't it? Come on now, I've got to know—'

For a moment or two she was content just to lie against him, while her nerves gradually eased into comparative quiet and coherence. Then pulling herself away, she shook her head, 'No, not really. It was something I saw—'

With his arm still supporting her, he led her to the door. 'What *did* you see, Aleyne?'

'I don't know that either,' she said. 'Perhaps it was just a—a hallucination. The fog was thick. Nothing was really clear. It *looked* like Yvonne. But it couldn't have been, could it?

She'd never say such things—?' Aleyne shook her head mutely, and seeing she was still confused, Adam took her into the lounge and forced a stiff brandy on her. She took it without demur, and began slowly to look better. But when he questioned her about the incident she either simulated forgetfulness, or really couldn't recall the details. All he got from her was 'I went out for a walk and had an attack of nerves, I suppose. Forgive me, Adam, for making such a "thing" of it. It was nothing.'

Just then Lucinda came in. 'Am I disturbing anything?' she asked with an edge to her voice.

Adam pulled himself together.

'Aleyne's had a bit of a shock.'

'What sort of shock? *Manfred?*'

'Lucinda—' Adam said warningly.

Lucinda laughed; a brittle sound.

'Oh come off it, Adam. You must know by now what a devil he is. And my sister's impressionable. Always was.' Her eyes softened momentarily, 'Poor darling. Come on, Ally, tell big bad Luce all about it—' She proffered a hand which Aleyne took mechanically.

Adam watched them speculatively as they went hand in hand out of the room.

Women, he thought wrily, he'd never understand them.

Lucinda possibly had more heart than he'd thought.

But why the sudden venom towards

Manfred?

An unreasoning jealousy slowly expanded in him, and a few minutes later hearing Lucinda's footsteps moving overhead along the landing to their own room he went upstairs purposefully, exhilarated yet half-ashamed of the uncontrollable lust that possessed him.

When he went in Lucinda was standing by the window staring out into the furred air, every line of her lovely body accentuated provocatively.

He paused by the bed.

She looked round.

'Come here,' he said meaningfully.

Astonishment flooded her eyes.

'But—'

'Come here, Lucinda,' he said thickly. 'You're my wife aren't you? You robbed me of Aleyne—'

'*Robbed* you? Adam what on earth's got into you? You must be mad. Don't look like that—'

She backed away, shocked by his expression which momentarily was not Adam's at all, but of something far more primitive and evil—a brute force emanating from ancient instincts far beyond the control of rational or human behaviour. A little cry left her lips as he bore down on them, then abruptly he released her, got up, and with his head in his hands went to the window. The perspiration was wet on her forehead, streaming down her neck over her whole body. A dark cloud seemed to fill the

102

room. When it had cleared he moved towards her again and took her hand.

'You must forgive me,' he said. 'I wouldn't harm you, you know. What got into me I can't think—'

His face was very pale.

When she spoke her voice sounded lifeless, without hope.

'*I* do, Adam.' She didn't say, 'It was Manfred.' Although the knowledge was there.

'What?'

'This place,' she told him. 'Perhaps we'd better leave.'

'We will,' he told her.

'When?'

A veiled look crossed his face. He loosened his collar nervously. Instinct told him they should pack up right away. But dogged reason insisted he should stay until at least some of the knots in the dark pattern of their life there were tied up or else exorcised. The queer aberration of his behaviour had been only temporary. In future he'd keep a firm control of himself so no harm came to any of them.

*   *   *

Meanwhile, at the Saunders' house, The Beeches, a queer lethargy, not entirely due to the pain of her ankle, had fallen upon the usually ebullient and commonsensical Rose.

'About that meeting, Hiram,' she said to her

103

husband, 'I guess there's not much point in it after all. If Manfred Hearne wants his Samain feast he'll have it, and nothing we can say will alter things. I don't see myself trudging round from house to house in this weather.'

'Of course not, love. Glad you've got back your commonsense,' Hiram answered. 'As I said, we needn't go.'

'I reckon we will, though,' Rose said quietly. 'Just like all the rest. It'd look funny—well, kind of cowardly—staying away if the others were there. And we don't want to cut ourselves off, do we?'

Hiram shrugged. 'It's up to you, midear. We'll do just what you want, when the time comes. It's only October, after all. A whole fortnight yet. In a fortnight a lot can happen.'

A true enough statement, but one which proved, in this case, erroneous. Because although everyone unknown to each other waited with nerves secretly taut for some occurrence to break the tension, nothing at all obvious happened. Manfred's piano was curiously silent, and Manfred himself showed a casual but beguiling friendliness to anyone he happened to meet.

Poppy confessed to Lloyd that perhaps after all they'd been mistaken about him.

'Maybe he's just a larger-than-life crank,' she said musingly. 'But then we're all a bit off-beat aren't we? And he does have *something*. You know—vitality. As for Mag-Mell—well,

104

what's wrong with acting the fool on occasion, like kids, I mean?'

Lloyd threw her an enigmatic glance.

'Don't tell me you're coming round to his plans? I thought you'd decided on no account to take part in Samain.'

'Oh, I've left an open mind,' Poppy said airily. 'I *never* make rigid decisions.' There was a pause, 'Except where you're concerned, of course,' and she giggled meaningfully.

Lloyd frowned.

'Don't be too sure of me,' he said with a hint of irritation. 'Or if you are, don't show it. That wouldn't be at all clever of you, Poppy. As I said—we share alike or not at all. Remember?'

Stifling a hot retort, Poppy nodded dumbly.

There was an awkward interim between them before Lloyd said surprisingly, 'You may be right about Manfred and possibly we'd be bloody idiots to turn down a bit of fun. So let's drink to it shall we?'

'To what? Our marriage?'

'And to Samain,' he said mockingly.

'To both then,' she agreed.

He fetched glasses with drinks from the cabinet and a moment later they were toasting the future.

Across the lane opposite a dark young form peered smiling.

And on a hummock above the wood three stark shapes of ancient elder trees stood twisted skeleton-like against the yellowing sky, naked black arms swaying fitfully in the rising wind.

CHAPTER EIGHT

Following Lucinda's brief suggestion for leaving Summerhayes, she let the matter drop, and gradually accepted that nothing would come of it. As matters settled into their former pattern, she realised she didn't really relish the thought. Secretly, like a knife twisting her nerves, a longing for revenge against Manfred grew and intensified—a longing to hurt him in some dark way as he had hurt and humiliated her. A glance of his eyes upon her—a sidelong look of insidious interest could still stir hidden pulses in her body; but they were the outcome of hatred more than desire. He might *think* he possessed her, but he didn't, any more than he possessed Bran. Bran, though his servant, was also something else—himself. What that was Lucinda was not sure. But the mere awareness between them was sufficient, to become a bond calculated one day to destroy Hearne's complete power.

Sometimes when Lucinda caught a glimpse of the boy gathering sticks for fuel from the wood, or standing with his back to her, arm outstretched towards a bird on a branch, swinging down the lane perhaps, in his

106

characteristic way, whistling, a queer maternal sense would stir in her. His neck was so slender and immature beneath the glistening dark curls. But when he turned abruptly, the startled eyes would be knowledgeable beyond his years, and she would be quickly shocked by the realisation that in many ways his wisdom far exceeded hers. Then she would be discomforted, ashamed of her longing to kiss and hold him.

Once when they met by chance, she forced herself to ask, 'How old are you, Bran?'

He regarded her with a wide-eyed frankness so calculated and prolonged it became almost a minute before replying.

'Old enough,' he said unsmilingly.

'For what?'

'I reckon you know; things.'

'No, I don't know,' she told him flushing. 'About nature, is that it? The earth, animals, growing things?'

He shrugged.

'Take it any way you like, lady. I'm not the clever sort.'

'Oh but I think you are,' Lucinda nearly said, as he ambled away. And with a stab of longing the repressed unloved quality in her felt a quiver of anguish that even Bran, a mere youth—well hardly that—had decided she was not worth confiding in.

By then she had grown almost reconciled to Adam's inward rejection. It had been obvious during the last two months at Summerhayes that though he made attempts at intervals of professed love, he didn't really care for her any more. She was useful as an antidote to Aleyne, but little more. When he took her in passion she guessed with uncanny instinct he was pretending she was her own half-sister. No doubt he would act honourably, according to his fashion, but she felt deeply, instinctively, that the bond between them was fundamentally sterile. Adam wanted children, but, though he might gull himself into thinking so, he did not want hers.

It was Aleyne—always Aleyne. She should have known of course, from the very beginning; but during the first days of their coming together and his capitulation everything had been such fun, a game and a challenge she couldn't resist. It had been habitual with her to ensnare men, and Adam had proved to be more irresistible than most. As a lover their relationship might have worked. But a husband? She knew now, he never really had been. Morally and emotionally he was Aleyne's.

She'd won in getting him for herself, but the victory was bitter, leaving only the hollow vacuum of dead-sea-fruit in her veins. Sometimes she felt so bereft her anger irrationally flared against Aleyne. Then reason asserted itself. Honestly was perhaps her greatest virtue. Aleyne had loved and still loved Adam. If they'd only take off together or at least have the courage for an open flagrant affair she herself might not feel so badly about their present relationship. As it was—they would go on as they were, she supposed, pretending, lying hypocritically, playing a game of make-believe loyalties that had no basis in fact.

Manfred could have given her the explosive warmth to erase the chill of Adam's inward contempt. But Manfred had merely exploited and used her.

'I hate him—hate him,' her thoughts ran, 'wait till Samain. You just wait. Something will happen.'

During the last week of October a flurry of snow came, filming the lean trees and hedgerows with white. That same afternoon Lloyd and Poppy were married in Penzance unknown to their friends, and returned together to Poppy's residence which was considerably larger and more luxurious than Lloyd's.

'We must have a party,' Poppy announced, when both were well fortified with champagne. 'Tomorrow perhaps. We'll wander round in the morning and get news going. Oh boy, what a lark. And what a chin-wag there'll be—'

Lloyd grinned, as he pulled her into his arms. 'Forget the chin wagging,' he said throatily, 'and remember what we're here for my girl.'

One hand sensuously travelled the line of breasts and thighs, lingering perceptibly about the buttocks. Then he lifted her up and pressed his moist lips against the delicate hollow of her throat. She shivered, instinctively stiffening.

'Hey now, none of that,' Lloyd said meaningfully. 'This is where your education properly begins. Don't play the innocent on me, Poppy. You're mine now, and see you don't bloody well forget it.'

Was it her imagination, or did the room suddenly darken and thicken with cloying air? And was that really Lloyd speaking or—someone else?

Poppy was still shivering when he carried her upstairs to the bed; and afterwards when all was over, though sexually appeased, there was a faint dark shadow at the back of her mind.

'Lloyd—' she said as she lay with his arm loosely over her. 'Lloyd, do you think—' she broke off hesitantly.

He raised his head slightly. 'Yes? What?'

'Don't you think it would be rather nice to have a blessing first? *Before* the party I mean?'

Lloyd frowned.

'*Blessing*? What the hell do you mean?'

'In church. Oh I know we're properly married. Still, it *was* the registry office. And I love you so much it would be nice to think—I mean—'

110

'You mean you've gone religious all of a sudden?'

If his tones were contemptuous she did not notice.

'I was brought up Catholic,' she said a little tartly.

'Indeed? I'd never have guessed.'

'Oh I know it doesn't make any difference *really*. Still—' she stared at him pleadingly, 'to please *me*, darling?'

He sighed. 'I don't know what's got into you all of a sudden. Anyway there's no Catholic Church within *miles* of here.'

'That wouldn't matter. Any church would do. Magswikk. We could go and see the rector, couldn't we?'

Eventually Lloyd, realising Poppy was so determined about it and not wishing to upset the apple-cart before it was properly established, agreed. And the next morning, quite early, they set off for the village.

At the corner of the narrow drive leading to the Carsons' house they saw Emily swathed in a voluminous woollen purple cape that exaggerated her size unbecomingly. A hood fringed with white fur framed her plump cheeks. Although rosy she looked edgy. Poppy was about to explode the news of the marriage when Emily said in flurried tones, 'I'm just off to meet Freddie—at the corner you know—the main road. He should be back anytime—'

'Oh?' Poppy exclaimed, 'has he been away?'

111

'Just for the night,' Emily answered, adding explanatorily with an effort at dignity, 'a business matter.'

When they'd passed on Poppy remarked to Lloyd, 'How odd. It's the first time I've heard any reference to business where Freddie's concerned. Except perhaps—well, I *have* heard unofficially he's got a little floozie tucked away somewhere in Penzance. Poor Emily.'

'Who told you?'

Poppy winked. 'At the hairdresser's things get around. You've no idea how news can travel under those dryers. Of course it mightn't be true.'

Actually it was; and at the precise moment of Emily's reference to her husband's business, Freddie was slipping furtively from the arms of his yellow-haired amour, to quickly dress and get away in his car before 'poor old Emily' began to get any inconvenient ideas.

Had he only known it Emily already had plenty of them, which she preferred stoically to disregard rather than force to a point of confrontation. If Freddie had an occasional flutter with cards, racing, or girls, she told herself stubbornly, she could afford to make light of them. He was young, and she herself was no pin-up or ever had been. Looked on from the right angle she was a lucky woman. The only trouble was that her life seemed from such a viewpoint frequently rather depressing, and she couldn't help, as now, a vague unease that intensified unpleasantly as she passed some trees near the corner of the main road.

Her senses were momentarily blurred, with an unseen dark cloud gathering in a knot of jealousy at the back of her head. 'I'll not have it', she thought, with uncharacteristic anger. 'If he makes a fool of me I'll see he suffers. Not a penny of mine—' a fitful wind brushed a lock of her too-red hair against her face. Her pulse was hammering and for a few seconds it seemed the bushes and very earth itself echoed with the ugly chant—'I'll see he suffers—suffers—suffers—' then, abruptly, it ceased.

With difficulty she pulled herself together, and as her temper died the cloud was dispersed, and she walked on wondering what had got into her. Was it blood pressure or what? She'd have to have a check-up, that was certain. When Freddie got back she'd ask him to ring the doctor for an appointment, then there'd be no getting out of it. Doctors always mildly frightened her in case they discovered she had a bad heart or something. But her husband was constantly urging her to go. And that proved, didn't it, that deep down he was really very fond of her. Dear Freddie. It was wrong of her to let a single doubt of him confuse her stupid head.

She plodded on, and didn't see the face peering after her from the shadowed trees; a curiously alert sly face, dark and intently watchful, that could have been that of a boy or man—or of some unknown stranger with his own frightening game to play.

Meanwhile Poppy and Lloyd were nearing Magswikk.

The church caught a quiver of gold from frail sunlight penetrating the lowering sky, but on the opposite side the grey forbidding rectory was still swathed in shadow, pin-pointed with drifts of thin snow.

Near the gate of the drab garden Lloyd paused and said, 'Are you absolutely certain, Poppy?'

'About what?'

'This blessing carry-on. Looks a grim sort of place to me. How do we know the old sky-pilot will want to oblige?'

'Don't talk that way,' Poppy said sharply. '*Sky*-pilot. Besides he mayn't be old at all; or if he is we may find he's a cheery jolly soul like country parsons often are.'

Poppy of course was being over-optimistic, and although obsequiously polite, the rector, having shown them into the living-room and heard their request, was disappointingly uncooperative.

'I do appreciate your natural desire to be of the spiritual elect,' he said, walking to the window and back again with his hands clasped together, thumbs wide-spread against his black clad chest. 'But I'm sure you must realise when you've given a little thought to the matter that it is *quite* impossible—in *my* church, certainly.

114

We're a rather strict community here. A marriage outside the true faith cannot under any circumstances be accepted as a sacred union and as such, dear people, you must necessarily be deprived of the very high privilege accorded to our own blessed congregation. However—'

'Right. O.K. we understand,' Lloyd interrupted. 'Say no more. It was just an idea—of my wife's. As for me I've no room for such clap-trap anyway. So we'll be off.'

He pulled Poppy to her feet, jerking her towards the door. But as it had been with Adam, the tubby little figure was there first. He swung round, eyes blazing under fierce brows, lips contorted into a sneer of outrage.

'I will not suffer vilification on these premises, sir. In the old days sinners were burned at the stake or hanged for desecration of such a kind. Consider yourselves lucky to get off with a warning. And I *do* warn you that if any of your kind *dare* to trespass on these sacred premises again, they will have something to answer for. Something very serious indeed.'

When they were once more outside, Poppy, who was trembling, said, 'Do you know, Lloyd, I think he's mad. He must be. His face—at one point it seemed to—to expand. He looked just like some weird monstrous toad, or—'

'Don't malign toads,' Lloyd answered cryptically. 'They can be useful and quite

115

interesting in their place. But *that*—! Poppy, I did warn you. Now you've seen for yourself what religious hokum-pokum can be in these out-of-the-way places perhaps you'll drop your tom-fool notion of having a blessing.'

'I suppose I'll have to,' Poppy agreed surprisingly in rather abject tones. 'It was just an idea.'

They walked down the slope silently and as they turned the corner leading away from Magswikk a curious sense of discomfort fell on them. The sun had retreated behind the sullen clouds again, and the ground appeared blackish and wet between the thin layer of snow. Once Poppy inadvertently looked back. Lloyd felt her fingers tighten on his arm.

'Lloyd, look.'

He turned his head casually, wondering if the unsavoury tubby little gentleman of the cloth had made it his business to see them safely off the premises. The hummock of land was deserted of humanity. The roof tops of Magswikk emerged cold and aloof-looking from the dip below. All trace of sunlight was deadened now into leaden uniformity predicting further snow. The trees on the right loomed in inky shadow, and further back three isolated trunks stood bleak and unlovely with hungry twisted branches outstretched and bent.

Poppy shivered.

'It isn't nice round here, is it?' she said

116

involuntarily. 'I never noticed those—those things before.'

Lloyd laughed brusquely, though he too felt a pang of unease. 'You've never been on a day like this,' he said practically. 'The light can do strange things with the imagination as you should know being, I hope, an intelligent woman.'

Poppy sighed and momentarily rested her face against his shoulder.

'I hope you didn't marry me for intelligence,' she said unsteadily. 'I'm not really, you know.'

His arm squeezed her waist possessively. 'So you say. But you had enough of it to nab *me*, my love and of course the wherewithal which was a great help.'

Poppy glanced up sharply. '*Lloyd!* What a perfectly beastly thing to say. As if it was for what I'd *got*—'

She broke off in exasperation. His eyes when they studied her were veiled, colder than usual.

'Naturally it was for what you've got,' he said lightly, 'looks, charm and the rest. Only—don't go heavy on me, sweet. Remember? No chains.'

She agreed mutely. But as they continued along the lane it seemed that something had been spoiled. What before had been banter between them had now assumed real and rather frightening proportions. *Would* Lloyd have married her if she'd had nothing? She knew he wouldn't. She'd always been a realist despite her soft core of romanticism. In a way, then, she'd bought him.

She drew away sharply, wishing they'd never made the stupid visit to Magswikk. If she hadn't forced the religious issue the truth could have been left to slumber unconsciously at the back of her mind. What had started off such an unfruitful trend of thought? That horrid cleric of course, and the gloomy rectory and churchyard. All those neglected tombstones, standing like ghouls watching, and the evil trees. Yes, they were evil, those macabre grasping things. Everything suddenly seemed threatening and full of dread.

She quickened her pace, as Lloyd took her hand.

'Hey, cheer up,' he said, 'what's got into you? Come on now, it's our wedding day. Champagne. That's what you need and lots of it.'

They hurried on, through a rising wind holding a flurry of snow. Near Manfred's cottage there was a wild scream as a cat's lean shape leaped over the path. Poppy shuddered. Behind the window Manfred's large form watched them statically. With their heads bent against the thickening snow neither of them saw Yvonne Court tiptoeing in the shadow of the hedge towards Hearne's cottage. Her face was shrouded in the hook of her black macintosh cape, her eyes burning with jealousy under a straggle of yellowed hair. 'Nasty creatures,' she thought, 'vulgar things', and pictured them lying together as she longed to lie with Manfred—close, close—so close they became one not only in spirit but flesh.

'It will happen,' she told herself as she crept half bent towards Hearne's gate. 'One day he'll forget everything but *me*. Even the cat and that—that Bran. Wait till Samain. When Samain comes it will happen.'

A mad little chuckle escaped her.

When she knocked at the door with her thin fist, Manfred opened it.

A wide frog-like smile curved his face.

'Come in, my dear,' he said. 'A little treatment, yes?'

Yvonne nodded mutely.

Once in his sanctum, she sighed rapturously, and like a backward child who'd learned her lesson automatically, undressed and lay herself on the couch.

Hearne regarded her meagre form with distaste; but in his eyes also was malicious triumph as he started kneading her body, gently at first, increasing gradually in pressure until she screamed from delicious little stabs of pain.

On the top of the chest the cat, Sam, sat motionless watching with arrogant contempt.

Further up the lane the wood was quiet, except for a creaking of branches where a tall

119

dark form made his way to a central clearing. He was taut-muscled and lean, a stranger. No one saw him come or go, his eyes were turned to the ground, as though in concentration. Occasionally some small wild thing scurried away when he approached. Then he laughed. It was not a nice sound.

But Aleyne might have recognised it and recalled Beltane when fiery dark eyes had burned into her own, claiming what she was not prepared to give.

CHAPTER NINE

Days passed with an inexorable sense of fatalism towards Samain. Rose and Hiram, uncomfortably aware of the forthcoming event, toyed more than once with the suggestion of a 'trip to town', but abandoned the project because Rose, unaccountably, was suddenly hit by an attack of muscular rheumatism that made the journey seem impractical.

'Never mind,' she said optimistically, 'it'll keep me away from those fun and games, love—no one would expect me to sport about in the wood with creaking muscles—'

Her husband eyed her shrewdly. 'You never know, mi'dear, it could pass off as quickly as it came, anyway—why do we need an *excuse* for not turning up?'

'Morale, if you like,' Rose answered.

'You mean keeping up with the Joneses?'

'Nothing of the sort,' Rose answered sharply. 'The Joneses'—or whatever you like to call them—are way behind us in things that count and you know it; we may be self-made, Hiram, but we've made a damn good job of it. And don't you go forgetting it.'

Hiram agreed mutely, although he couldn't quite fathom what worldly status had to do with Hearne's off-beat festival. Like a crowd of elderly hippies or punks, we are, he told himself ironically. But he knew that if Rose had recovered in time for the party they'd go. Besides, there was a streak of hard-headed curiosity in him. He wanted to know what was going on, as any astute business man would, and if there was anything wrong get it put right. Certainly there was something unsavoury in the air and many a time, he wished he and Rose hadn't got so involved with a bunch of cranks. He didn't entirely discard the possibility of psychic phenomena, but he'd a shrewd idea their basis was mostly physical— something that could be explained away in perfectly practical terms once the key was found. Magic? The world was full of it. Look at those theatrical Johnnies with their mystifying acts; mind-readers too, spoon-benders and the like. Then the hypnotists who could sway whole audiences. He'd watched the last more

121

than once, and had remained outside it all—not felt a thing, although there'd been something weird in seeing such a crowd apparently under the influence of one other man's mind.

He always kept the word 'apparently' in the forefront of his thoughts. Folks liked to be fooled sometimes—it gave a zest to life. And as long as you were aware of it he couldn't see it did any harm. Anyway science was the answer nowadays to a great deal of queer happenings. You had television, hadn't you, produced by electrical unseen waves and impulses—there were wavelengths everywhere capable of projecting pictures and atmosphere once you had the know-how. Manfred Hearne had obviously made it his business to dabble in conning folks' minds as well as bodies. A womaniser too, and a not very nice one. That tune they fell for—nothing particularly pleasant about it, but then it wasn't really the tune that got them, it was the man. And another point was the drink; Hearne's bloody-special brew. Manfred was astute enough to get them all pretty high before any party business started. Hiram had discovered himself how potent it was, though not being a connoisseur of off-beat high-falutin wines and spirits, he couldn't place the stuff. There was a hint of elder-flower about it and something much stronger, probably loaded with some obnoxious drug. Well, at the Samain business—if they went—he'd see that Rose and himself somehow steered clear of the preliminaries. So, buoyed up by his own commonsense reasoning, he allowed himself to take the course of least resistence, knowing that this was what Rose also wanted.

With the Carsons it was different. Under a veneer of light-heartedness put on for her husband's benefit, Emily steeled herself with increasing foreboding for the feast. Once she'd ventured to suggest it was rather silly for adult people to be drawn into such 'goings on'. Freddie's reaction had been not only instantaneous but shatteringly rude. 'All right, do what you like. Stay brooding at home if you want,' he'd said, with a contempt in his voice he'd not have dared to use in their earlier days. *'I'm* going and that's that. Not much excitement and fun round here at the best of times, and if you think I'm going to miss any for the sake of looking at television or your face all evening, you've another thing coming.'

Emily was so outraged she had to steady herself against the table to keep from falling. The blood pounded through her arteries, against her ribs and ear-drums; at the same time a wave of suffocating darkness seemed to enclose the room, conveying a terror so intense she thought, 'I'm dying—or else it's a stroke— and all that money, the will he made me write—' one plump hand went up to her throat. She closed her eyes briefly, and when she opened them again the darkness was already lifting. Freddie was bearing over her with a queer look in his narrowed eyes. 'As if he wants me dead—' her mind ran; 'dead, *dead*, so he can be with that little whore—'

She tried to say something, but the words wouldn't come. Instead he spoke:

'O.K., old girl?' he asked. 'What's up, eh? Faint or something?'

She shook her head. 'I'm all right. It was—'

'Thinking of the party?' He smiled enigmatically. 'Well, it's up to you, isn't it? I was a bit blunt perhaps, I suppose I was disappointed.'

'Disappointed?'

'That you won't be there. A pity. Never mind. I wouldn't want you to come if you weren't up to it, you know that, don't you, Em?'

'I shall be there,' she said, rather coldly. 'Don't worry.'

He turned for the drinks' cabinet and, though she couldn't see his scowl, she knew it was there.

A minute later he returned with a stiff whisky. 'There you are. Drink it up. Maybe you should see the doctor sometime for a check.'

So he wanted to frighten her she thought. Doctors, check-ups—and he knew she fretted about palpitations. Well, she wasn't going to give him the satisfaction this time.

'Don't worry,' she said firmly. 'I'm as strong

124

as an ox,' continuing a moment later with a playfully simulated smile, 'I can assure you, dear boy, your expectations aren't likely to be realised for quite some time yet.' She did not add 'perhaps never' although she thought it.

Her husband left the room rather abruptly. Emily went to the window. The light was dying. Up the lane she thought she saw a figure striding towards the shadowed trees. He was tall and slender, very dark against the falling evening. 'Funny,' she said to herself, 'I've never seen *him* before. Obviously a stranger. Probably a tinker of some kind.'

He was soon gone. At the same moment a cat screamed, followed by the slowly rising wail of Manfred Hearne's concerto.

At Summerhayes Aleyne heard it. She was laying the table in the lounge for the evening meal. Her stomach and nerves lurched, with the quickening of her heart. What was he saying? What did he want? Why did the image of his form rise suddenly before her mind's eye? So compellingly masculine and desiring? Magnetic and overpowering, yet hateful at the same time?

She forced herself from the window with her hands tightly clenched at her sides. Adam came into the room unexpectedly.

She made a little rush towards him, and was taken into his arms, while the sobs rose in her throat, heaving thickly against his chest.

'Oh, Adam—Adam—help me—'

His hand stroked her hair. She could feel his body tauten then melt in sympathy and warm desire.

'There—there—my poor sweet love—' the tones were a mere whisper and perhaps Lucinda did not hear as the door opened with a snap.

They were apart when she entered, but her eyes held a derisive glint.

'Braving it together?' she said.

'What?' Adam snapped.

She lifted an arm. 'That thing. The tune.'

'I didn't notice anything,' he said stiffly.

'Oh come now!' Lucinda's grimace was ironic. 'You're such a bad liar, Adam. Anyway—' Her eyes rested briefly, with a touch of malice on her sister. '*Ally* did. You'd better keep a firm hold of her, darling, or she'll be off like a puff of wind to the magician's lair.'

'Don't be silly,' Aleyne said. 'If it's Manfred you're talking about—'

'Of *course* it's Manfred. Who else? Look at you—all white and shaken—'

'For heaven's sake, Lucinda, leave Aleyne alone,' Adam told her almost roughly, adding after a perceptible pause, 'and I don't think *you're* in a position to talk. At Beltane it was pretty obvious what you were aiming for—'

'Ah. But Beltane's over,' Lucinda's voice was sly, smug, a little taunting. 'And things are different now.'

'What do you mean?'

'I mean, Adam dear, that any lingering secret attraction I felt for him is well and truly exorcised. Dead; quite dead.'

Aleyne shivered.

'He's a bore and a beast,' Lucinda continued. 'Not only that—dangerous to anyone weak-minded enough to fall for his tricks. And he's got his eye on Ally. So if I were you I'd keep her at any cost from going to this Samain business. You know what it means, don't you? Samain?' She smiled knowingly. 'I've been reading about it in a book Adam has upstairs. Samain, according to Celtic tradition, was the period when ghosts and witches walked in olden times. Beltane was the time when the earth woke after its long winter sleep and fires were lit to ensure the renewal of life.' She paused, adding after a second or two, 'So you see, we should *all* be a bit careful, shouldn't we?' Though her voice was light her eyes were guarded, strained; her whole posture appeared to have stiffened as though ready to face some confrontation ahead.

Adam viewed her uneasily. Then he said, 'If you feel like that, Lucinda, it might be better for *you* to stay at home.'

'You mean you've quite decided you're really going?'

'Yes. I mean just that. I'm not afraid of a lusting wily bastard like Hearne, or of any other so-called mystic or dabbler in dark things. I'm not deceiving myself either that it's a healthy pursuit trying to unmask witches and warlocks. But if they do exist—even as projections merely of a warped mind—then it's better to know about it. Running away's no good.'

'Yes, I agree with you,' Aleyne said quietly.

'And me,' Lucinda remarked, having regained composure. 'So that's settled. We go, and I shall make a night of it—have fun. I've got that thick woolly Kaftan thing—at least it's not *really* wool—but you've seen it, haven't you, Ally?—All embroidered down the front, and with lots of beads and berries in my hair, I shall be a sort of woodland witch, and call all the doomed and dead to life—ooh!—'

'Lucinda, *don't*—' Aleyne cried rather shrilly. '*Please* don't make fun of things—'

Lucinda stared at her, brows raised in astonishment. '*Fun*? Why not? If we didn't make fun we'd be—'

'Yes?'

'Lost, I'd think, quite lost,' Lucinda said, with an abrupt change of mood. 'And Adam knows it.'

She swept out of the room abruptly, leaving Adam and Aleyne staring after her.

The door closed.

Across the carpet a shadow streaked, not clearly defined, but in a zig-zagged shape of pointed angles suggesting a hunched form with grotesque features and grasping claws. A second later it had faded, leaving a chill behind that even the cheerful leaping of flames from the fire did not for minutes dispel.

Aleyne shook her head despondently.

'I just don't know,' she said with her face turned from Adam.

'Know what?'

'Why we've got into it—you, me, Lucinda, Yvonne, the Walshes—even Rose and Hiram—all of us. It's become a *thing*, hasn't it, this business of old rites and magic. A sort of hysteria. When Manfred Hearne says "Jump" we jump. When he whispers "Walk into my parlour"—' she broke off with a sigh that became suddenly a shudder.

'Now *you're* being a bit melodramatic, aren't you?' Adam said rather shortly. 'At first it was Lucinda. But for some reason she's changed. Oh not about the set-up—she's got the atmosphere all right. But Hearne.'

Aleyne remained silent.

'I wonder why now?' Adam resumed. 'At Beltane she was besotted with the man. Now I really don't think she cares a damn. Why? That's the point?'

Aleyne shrugged.

'Does it matter? You should be pleased. She's probably come to her senses and fallen in love with you all over again.'

'*Again?*'

'Oh yes,' Aleyne admitted with a wry, half-sad note in her voice. 'I think she *did*—does love you, Adam. She's not entirely a bitch you know. A lot of her brashness is put on. Underneath there's a streak of insecurity in her. That's why she has to prove herself—'

'Now you're being kind.'

'No. Honest. I've been looking into myself lately, quite a bit, secretly. At the time, when you married Luce, I was bitter. I blamed her entirely. Now I know if you'd cared for me enough you wouldn't have even thought about her. So it's not fair to make her the scapegoat. Anyway—I should have fought more.'

'I've wondered sometimes why you didn't.'

'Pride, Adam, which proves I hadn't got what it takes, doesn't it?'

'I don't know what you mean.'

She smiled wanly. 'I should have been more of a tigress and shown my claws.'

Adam frowned and walked to the window. The shape of his head set so squarely on the broad shoulders filled her with an anguish of longing. Then he said without turning round, 'You're not the sort to have claws, Aleyne. That's one of the things I like about you.'

'*Like?*'

'Yes, *yes,*' he retorted, with a swing towards her. 'Passion's not all that rare between a man and woman, but *liking* is. You could call it, I suppose, a quality of loving.'

'Perhaps you're right.'

'I know I am. So it's done *one* thing for us at least—'

'*What* has? What do you mean?'

'Coming here. Beltane and the rest. Uncovered a few down-to-earth home truths about ourselves. And that's damn funny, isn't it? Down to earth.'

'I don't see anything funny, I'm afraid,' Aleyne remarked.

'No. It was the wrong word. Significant, I should have said. The *earth*, Aleyne. It's got *power* round here. Call me a crank if you like, but this land is *different*. Verdant, but primitive somehow. Retaining a whole heap of past emotions and macabre happenings beneath the surface. Well, why not? It could be a perfectly rational and scientific explanation. And if that's the truth Hearne's merely been a bit brighter than the rest of us, and found a way of conjuring up the—'

'Dead?'

'No. Just a reflection.'

'Whatever it is, it's not very pleasant. And I don't agree with your *dead* theory. Oh, Adam, let's drop this conversation. With Samain in the offing, couldn't we try for a bit of normality in the meantime?'

He took her hand. She could feel her palm pulsing against his. Her whole body was suddenly alight, though she tried not to show it.

'Of course,' he said.

But secretly he doubted that. Until the ridiculous festival business was over, the word normal was mere wishful thinking.

CHAPTER TEN

The day before the festival was fine. Manfred either personally or by notes delivered by Bran informed residents they'd be expected in the wood shortly before four-thirty, the following evening.

He took acceptance for granted, adding with a knowing glance at Adam, 'Tomorrow will be the moment of truth, old man. If you feel like facing it turn up. If you don't, steer clear of the affair. I've a good hunch the women will be there.'

So had Adam. In spite of Lucinda's professed newly acquired aversion to Hearne it was obvious she was stimulated. Aleyne, too, was more curious and titivated by the business than she admitted. 'Titivated' though was hardly the word, Adam thought ironically; 'haunted' was nearer to the mark. Haunted and in a queer way afraid. Not that he blamed her. The fellow had an insidious dominance that could be best described as 'unholy'—a quality probably possessed by the notorious Alasteir Crowley, who in his time had been described as the arch villain of the Black Arts. How much of *his* power had been the devil's and how much entirely physical was a debatable point. Adam had a shrewd idea it was the latter, combined with the unsavoury

132

gift of resurrecting elemental impressions from certain areas of the earth's surface. He didn't accept any such emanations could harm, unless the 'victim'—and what an apt word under the circumstances—was in a state of highly strung emotional acceptance or extreme terror. In this case there had to be a partnership and he was damned if he was going to see Aleyne initiated as one of Manfred's 'spiritual' harem. Spiritual? Mag-Mell? What a laugh. Against his will though, Adam's mind was invaded, as it had been frequently, by the obnoxious image of Aleyne's possible capitulation to Hearne's animal magnetism. There were moments when he was tortured by the knowledge of her vulnerability, and cursed himself for having deserted her for Lucinda. If she'd been his wife, there'd have been no conflict, no danger. Aleyne was single-minded. Devotion like hers, when snapped at the root, could spring dangerously in two directions. It should have been her safeguard. But shock and doubt had shattered the very foundations of her existence. The blame was his.

Many times he'd toyed with the thought of sending her away—telling her brutally, she was not wanted at Summerhayes—anything to force her from the constant battle of warring good and evil in which he'd become so involved. But his courage had failed. Quite probably Aleyne would have thrown his own words back in his face with some bitter comment that would shame him.

The problem remained.

He still wanted her.

Wanted her that night before Samain so achingly he buried himself fiercely with all the lust that was in him in the heady lusciousness of Lucinda's available body.

His wife, being Lucinda, responded, although a veiled mockery clouded her eyes afterwards, and her voice was cool when she said, 'Hungry tonight, aren't you, darling? Getting yourself well armoured up?'

He drew away, staring at the ceiling.

'Well?' Lucinda prompted, edging closer, 'is that it?'

The perfume of her hair and body distracted him. 'Lucinda, for heaven's sake. Just be quiet, will you?'

'And suppose I don't *want* to be quiet?' She sat up suddenly, tossing her luxuriant hair behind her ears over her shoulders. Her cheeks had warmed to a bright glow, her eyes were brilliant with anger when she continued, 'As I've said before, you treat me like a—like a—well, *you* know what. You have me whenever you feel like it and yet you can't even put on a pretence of civility afterwards. I asked you a *question*, Adam.'

'And a damn silly one. It's the wrong time for words if I may say so.'

She stared at him sullenly.

'Come on now—' to please her he let his lips brush over one bare shoulder. 'Go to sleep, Lucinda, try and rest.'

She suddenly relaxed and fell away from him.

'You're so cocksure,' she whispered. 'Men!—you're all alike.'

He didn't reply, except for a low-keyed 'mm—' And she knew he was already half-asleep.

But Lucinda didn't sleep. She lay for a long time watching the shadowed pattern of the moonlight streak the ceiling. Everything, presently, except for the sound of Adam's heavy rhythmic breathing, was uncannily quiet. There was no tapping of a tree against the window, no creak of undergrowth from outside. The complete silence was somehow ominous. Glancing at the luminous dial of her watch, she saw that the hands were at two-thirty. Impelled by instinct and curiosity she got out of bed and went to the window. The garden below lay cold and frosted in the luminous light, holding the peculiar quality of a world half-dream out of time. There was no cloud streaking the face of the moon. On such a night phantoms could walk, and tombs give up their dead.

Lucinda shivered. She was not normally an imaginative person and with an effort she pulled her nerves together, telling herself she was letting the Samain business get on top of

135

her. Then, gradually, the shadows cast by the bushes at the gate appeared to part, revealing a face—pale and pointed, and weirdly compelling—the face of the boy, Bran, staring up at her. In a streak of moonlight his features were vividly clear—dark watchful eyes slanted slightly upwards, thin beautifully formed lips tilted in a knowing smile. She didn't move, but stood perfectly still, like a marble statue carved to immobility, with one hand holding the curtains a little apart.

The interim was brief, but electric, with an ancient atavistic knowledge stirring in communion between them.

What the message was, she couldn't tell. But she knew it was of intense significance, which the next day Samain would somehow resolve.

For a second she closed her eyes involuntarily; when she opened them again he was gone. There was nothing anymore but the fingered shadows streaking the grass, and the skeleton black branches of the trees standing stark against the greenish sky.

From the distance the faint sounds of a piano gradually rose mournfully, then died into silence as a quiver of wind shivered through the air.

With her hands to her ears, Lucinda forced herself back to bed.

Adam was *still* sleeping soundly.

At other times she would have snuggled in beside him. But for once a faint cold contempt seized her. There was no subtlety in him, no light or shade, or love—for her. It no longer worried her. Not that night. One image alone registered—the lithe young form and face of Bran—of youth eternal.

Mag-Mell.

Could it really be? She wondered musingly. Well, tomorrow they would know.

With this certainty in her, she slipped into bed and was presently asleep.

No one saw a tall shape moving through the wood that night, and if anyone had, there'd have been no recognition, except perhaps by Aleyne, and Aleyne was dreaming other things.

*   *   *

The next morning was cold but fine. Any slight wind there'd been during the night had died, and the wood was a shrouded mass of dark trunks immersed in grey shadows. Bran was about early, carrying logs to the clearing for the fire later. Yvonne spent an hour meditating at sunrise before making her way to Manfred's cottage for instructions. She had already prepared dishes for the feast, including salads containing special herbs and portions of tasty edible fungi, which had been thinly sliced and sprinkled with condiments. The special dressing was bottled, and the wine decanted; ivy had been picked and put ready coiled in a basket for festooning the trees. There was mistletoe too; Yvonne had made a wreath of it for herself, to go with a thick green velvet dress embroidered all over in a pattern of oak leaves.

Manfred, she knew, would be wearing a crown of some kind! But when she'd asked coyly if she couldn't have a peep at his costume, the sudden look of concentrated dislike on his face had withered her to abject apologising.

With her knuckles clenched over her thin breast, she'd said, 'I'm sorry, Manfred—I shouldn't have asked. I'm sorry—'

'Either call me "Master" or Mr Hearne,' he'd said contemptuously, adding more quietly, with a faint sardonic smile, 'you must not forget your place, my dear, must you?'

His broad countenance had seemed to swell and fill the room. He'd lifted a hand to her chin and tilted her face up to meet the compelling stare of his eyes. The lids were raised, revealing pin-points of pupils that expanded and dilated each second, draining life and energy from her.

'No—' she'd whispered, 'no—Master.'

His hand had closed on her shoulder, not fiercely, but with insidious suggestive gentleness.

'Run away then. Be a good girl, and there may be a treat in store later.'

Smiling warily, and shivering, with jaws

138

chattering and an animal-like servitude in her eyes she'd nodded and scurried off.

Hearne had laughed to himself as the door closed, thinking, 'But the treat, my dear, may not be at all to your liking.' Women! what fools they were—especially the sterile virgins who had neither sex nor passion to give—only a mute ridiculous obedience which at the most merely added a fraction to his power.

Actually his assessment of Yvonne was slightly off the mark. Under her cringing veneer were emotions so concentrated, her frail form shook with them like invisible wires suddenly pulled taut with each heart-beat.

Her desire for him was neither entirely lust or love, but a force battling within her body with the pent-up energy of a damned stream about to burst its banks.

Intermittently that day as she went about her duties concerning Samain she would pause rigidly, muttering to herself, 'I want him—*want* him. He is mine, *mine*.' Then after a short pause, her limbs would move again, jerkily automatically; and she'd go about her business only half-conscious of her actions.

Once in the afternoon she met Lucinda who was on her way to post some letters in the box on the hill overlooking Magswikk. As usual Lucinda was looking particularly exotic, wearing a white three-quarter length fur coat and hood, with fitting knee-length boots. She appeared slightly startled when Yvonne appeared round a corner by the wood.

'Oh—' she said, 'hullo. Nice day—' her voice trailed off uncertainly. Something in the other woman's manner disconcerted, almost affronted her.

Yvonne looked so queer—almost mad, she thought, with her hair hanging bedraggled over her shoulders, her pale eyes screwed up in her drawn face, chin thrust forward from her narrow neck.

'Where are you going?' she said suddenly, side-stepping in front of Lucinda.

Lucinda laughed. 'What's the matter? What business is it of yours?'

Yvonne put a hand to her forehead, swayed slightly, but as Lucinda made a gesture to help, she recovered, drew herself to a rigid stance of dignity and said, 'Of course not. You're quite right. Obviously—'

'Yes?'

'You've letters for the post. Shall I take them for you?'

'No thank you,' Lucinda answered. 'I'm out for a walk.'

'But—'

'Yes?'

'*That* way. Past the wood. And today of *all* times.'

'Oh I see. You mean Samain. When the ghoulies and ghosties take their airing. Look— you're taking things too seriously, Yvonne. Adam and I were only saying the other day—'

140

'*You? Adam?* What do *you* know about it? And don't mock. I was only trying to help— and now, if you'll excuse me, I have a call to make.' Yvonne pushed by abruptly, leaving Lucinda hesitating and looking back for a few moments. Then, as the thin figure in its flapping cape turned a bend half-hidden by trees, Lucinda jerked herself to movement, and continued walking quickly towards the post box. Whether Manfred saw her when she passed his cottage she didn't know. She resisted an impulse to glance that way, concentrating her attention on the other side of the lane.

Suddenly, quite irrationally, a terrible welling up of fear possessed her. The clear sky seemed to lower and the immediate surroundings assume gathering clarity and intensity. The post box stood only fifty yards or so away, but on the barren stretch of land bordering the wood ahead, the three stricken elder trees loomed increasingly malevolently clear against the winter sky. Lucinda's heart lurched, then raced sickeningly for a second or two, as the macabre forms seemed to take on an alien life of their own, clawing towards her with malignant purpose.

She rubbed her eyes, telling herself her sight was wrong; she must see an optician and have a proper test. The aberration was only momentary. When she looked up once more the blackened shapes were as they'd always been, mere static trunks and twisted branches spoiling an otherwise normal view.

Normal?

But was it?

Still trembling Lucinda glanced towards the hummock of land ahead to her right, above the village. She'd never noticed before how deserted and forbidding the church looked, or the unwelcome morbid appearance of the looming grey rectory facing it. The squares of windows appeared unusually dark and deserted. But in a beam of transient light that quivered momentarily then died again, a squat black-clad figure appeared to be watching her with an intentness she found curiously unnerving.

Was the whole place bewitched? Or was she letting her imagination play tricks? *She* of all people, who'd always considered herself so sophisticated and worldly-wise.

Laughing aloud, to restore a sense of equanimity, she hurried on and pushed the letters through the box; but shivers of fear still pulsed in her body. As she made her way back to Summerhayes she wished she'd told Adam she'd decided not to go to Samain that night. But to draw back now would be cowardly and an affront to her pride. She'd no intention of letting Aleyne be one up on her! Aleyne, she knew, would be present.

Besides, there was Bran.

Forcing other darker images from her mind

she revisualised his pointed young face and
slant eyes—his tilted mouth and glint of white
teeth when he smiled, his graceful slim body
with bare brown legs below the shabby tunic-
thing he wore. Ridiculously, the picture
brought a lump of emotion to her throat,
perhaps that was what she needed—a child, a
son of her own, created from some union
richer and more potent than her marriage to
Adam.

Adam.

Thinking of him restored all her old
cynicism. Her walk became more jaunty, she
looked completely her old self when she
reached the house. No one would have
guessed the ordeal she'd been through; least of
all Adam, who observing her from an upstairs
window as she walked up the path, had to
admit wrily, she certainly had style.

CHAPTER ELEVEN

Aleyne had decided to put on no frills or fancy
costume for the event, but to wear her green
woollen cape over a full peasant skirt of the
same shade, with a white sweater. She'd have
her hair loose under a headscarf, in this way
retaining her own identity. No flowers, no
beads, no ornate concessions to Manfred
Hearne's absurd ideology. She doubted even

143

that she'd taste his wine or food. The reason for her going at all would be mostly because Adam was. He was so dead set on proving or *dis*proving his own theory concerning Hearne's occult powers that she knew nothing anyone said would dissuade him.

Even if she wanted to. And she was not sure of that. The queer sense of other-worldness, of being drawn into another sphere of being, still overcame her at odd moments, when a sense of fatalism possessed her, and will-power seemed drained away, especially through the insidious melody of Hearne's concerto.

Mag-Mell? Tir-Na-Noc? How could a whole group of people have become involved in such a fantasy? Over and over again the question returned, to be dismissed with no answer. This fact in itself was frightening, in view of an apparent complete incapacity to deal with the spreading evil or in anyway stem its expanding tide.

If only it would rain, Aleyne thought, as the day progressed from its cold bright beginning towards winter sunshine. If only some unpredictable storm would rise to shatter the forthcoming event.

But by midday everywhere was filmed by motionless mellowing gold with no trace of a cloud in the sky. The air, though so quiet, seemed filled with a vibrant expectancy which escaped no one, though none admitted it. Poppy made one or two lighthearted comments to Lloyd which he answered with a short derisive laugh. Hiram treated the whole thing as a load of tomfoolery—or professed to. The Saunders were a little withdrawn about the matter, although Emily said once with simulated nonchalance, 'It's a good thing we're going, Hiram. It would've been a mistake to let the others think we were scared. I can see that now. After all it's only a game—a silly one I guess, but it'll soon be over.'

'What are you going to wear, Rose?'

'My mink,' Rose said, very deliberately. 'We didn't put all that down just for a coat to be hung in a wardrobe. I shall wear my fur hood too.'

Hiram winked. 'With a pair of pointed ears or horns stuck on?'

'Don't be silly, love. I don't intend to pander. Anyway—' she gave him a roguish smile, '—it wouldn't make sense, would it? A couple of Charlies we looked last time, and don't say anyone could've been gulled into taking me for a nymph.'

'No, thank heaven,' Hiram agreed. 'But that don't mean you can't be quite an eyeful when you're togged up. I shall have to keep a watch on Hearne tonight.'

Rose giggled. 'Go on you; don't be daft.'

Her tone was light; but at the back of her mind, though she wouldn't have admitted it, a small niggling shadow persisted giving her the curious feeling of acting a part in a charade, with someone or something always watching from just behind her shoulder.

With the Carsons it was quite different. Freddie had made a point of sending for a costume from some theatrical firm in Bristol, meant to represent a mythological woodland god. It was almost entirely composed of simulated fur and leaves, and Emily felt a sinking of her heart when she saw him wearing it. He really *did* appear quite handsome in a slim stagey way. The wreath of oak leaves round his head hid his already fading hair-line, giving him a majestic quality he certainly, in real life, did not possess. The short tunic gave a graceful view of his slim thighs which were encased in tightly fitting leather for warmth. The toes of the boots were slender, pointed and elongated. He could have been not a day over thirty.

But how was she going to compete with him, or rather live up to his new vision of youthfulness? It was as though she had received a slap in the face.

'Well, Freddie,' she said, careful not to appear at all resentful, 'you look very splendid, and I'm sure no one else will hold a candle to you. The problem is, what am *I* going to do?'

'*You*, my dear? How do you mean?'

'*Dress*,' she said more sharply than she'd intended. 'If we're going as a couple I should put on something suitable—something as much like yours as possible.'

As Freddie's back was turned to her she did not see the rising flush colour his face.

'We haven't necessarily to go as a couple,' he replied coldly. 'Husbands and wives should be independent sometimes—especially when it comes to style. After all you're hardly a Miranda or Titania. Just follow your own shape, Emily, wear the best you've got, with perhaps a few berries stuck out of one ear.'

How *cruel* of him, Emily thought with the sullen rising of anger she'd felt so often lately. And to mention her *shape*. Probably he was comparing her all the time with his tarty little dolly-bird in Penzance. And if she'd not made it clear to him she was going to Samain, he'd no doubt have somehow smuggled her over to the scene. It was unfair. *Frightful*—after all she'd done for him. Her vision clouded momentarily. The room seemed to revolve and quiver into a spreading vortex of darkening terror. If she swayed fitfully he did not notice. A few seconds later it was over. With her hands tightly clenched at her sides she managed to remark a little thickly, 'Just as you say. I'll see what I've got.'

But it was sometime before she could wipe the wave of hatred from her mind and thudding pulses. And as she sorted through her wardrobe, trying to make a final decision what to wear, desolation encompassed her. 'What's the point?' she thought miserably. 'I might as well be dead. No one wants me—*no*

147

one.'

If she could have cried it would have been easier, released some of the tension. But by the time she'd chosen a woollen buttercup coloured long dress with a voluminous bell-sleeved russet coat to go over it, all feeling had died in her. It would have been infinitely easier for her to have changed her mind and decided to have an evening in bed with a book. But the stubborn streak in her would not allow it. One thing was sure, she was not going to let her husband win that way.

*   *   *

The hours passed.

By three-thirty all was ready in the wood.

At his cottage Manfred sat at his piano playing.

The music, weird and mournful, but strangely compelling, whined through rooms and corridors, rising to an insidious haunting crescendo before fading again almost to a whisper—a mere plaintive sigh. His hands paused and hesitated on the keys, while complete silence claimed the room. In a dark corner two emerald pin-points of light gazed unblinkingly and motionlessly from a triangular feline face. Manfred's expression was enigmatic, concentrated on other things.

Presently he got up and went to the window. A sardonic look of contemptuous amusement

148

crept to his eyes when he saw Yvonne Court trudging past the gate with further greenery under her arms. What meagre grace she might once have possessed had become now a grotesque travesty of femininity. Little more than a bag of bones, he thought, dressed up in her tawdry finery—good company for those three black elders on the hill. Wouldn't surprise him at all if she didn't soon join them. Well—that wouldn't worry him. Her uses for him were now over. Complete servitude always bored him in the end, and when that happened he soon found means of getting that kind out of the way. In the meantime let her have her evening, of tripping and grimacing and jumping about when she was told to. She might even be of some assistance in providing a wedge between Aleyne and the enemy—Adam.

Oh yes, he was under no illusions just where he stood there. The man was out to thwart him. And Adam was no fool; he'd kept a keen watch on his sister-in-law because he was besotted by her. But there were things he didn't know; secrets of ancient knowledge of which he, Manfred, was master. And eventually the dark knowledge would win, be supreme. Aleyne, the tantalising lovely little madam, would be as subservient to his will as the stupid Yvonne. Already, when he closed his eyes, his mind was ravishing her. He could feel his pulses spring and bound. His fingers tingled with the urge to take her—to have her soft limbs entwined with his, while her body thrilled with the secret elixir only he could give. The moment of culmination would be supreme—timeless, above all physical laws of man. After that her eyes would see no one but him, her senses long for nothing else but to be his subject and slave.

His witchling.

And if she rebelled he would chastise her, until she begged for mercy. Then he would claim her in passion again, and she would be adoring and ready once more for mating and for blossoming as all living things struggled and flowered from the dark earth's primitive heart.

Thus fortified and complacent in his own powers, he left the window and went upstairs to dress for the festival. His costume meant to represent Llyr, was a fur tunic to be worn with his crown of felt oak leaves from which antlers rose in front. His ram-headed serpent-like sceptre carved by Bran would be his symbol of authority. All should worship him; *all*. Most would be gratified too, when the rites of Samain were properly established. And if his one rival rebelled he could be made the sacrifice. To savour Samain adequately it was essential there should be a victim of some kind. Yvonne would go her own mad way to destruction anyway. But Adam! ah—there would be reason in that; gratification in seeing him not one of the honoured, but of the doomed—an outcast condemned forever to the dark dead kingdom of Scathack, at the mercy of Ysbaddan and his legions of phantoms and horrors.

No Tir-Na-Noc or Mag-Mell for him; just—extinction.

A large smile unwittingly crossed Manfred's face. His appearance, when fully dressed, pleased him. But before leaving the cottage he slipped a black cloak over his form, and hid the antlered crown under it. No one must have an inkling of his true identity until he appeared on the scene surprisingly, at the precise moment when all were assembled in the clearing waiting to receive him.

Half stooping, he plunged down his path through the front gate and across the lane, cutting up in the shadows of the hedges to the wood. There was a hidden dark grove on the left, where Bran was already waiting. Everything by now was shrouded by quickly falling twilight, but a red glow filtered through the trees in the distance, blurred by smoke and shadows.

The boy stood erect and watchful, his slant eyes smouldering in his face. If a faint smile of derision touched his lips fleetingly, Hearne did not notice it, or could not have seen. The shadow cast by his own great form reduced all other shapes and details to negation.

'Is everything ready, Bran?' he asked.

'Yes, Master. Just as you wanted.'

'And—the guests?'

'They're there.'

'All of them?'

Bran nodded. 'Yes.'

'Good, good. Then help me into this thing, will you?'

Manfred handed the boy his headdress and slipped the black cloak from his shoulders. Expressing no word of approval or surprise the boy manipulated the crown into a proper position, and Hearne, drawing himself to his full height which assumed giant dark proportions in the veiled light, waited a few moments before moving into the shroud of massed trees.

Bran did not follow immediately, but stood musingly with one arm encircling the slim trunk of a young larch. What twilight remained slipped suddenly into static night. Muted sounds of voices came from the clearing while tongues of rosy flame intensified through the interlaced tracery of trees.

Bran suddenly roused himself and with a skipping motion disappeared in the direction of his 'master'. Eyes bright as emeralds followed. There was a wild cry and the fleeting shape of a lean feline form passing. Then all except for the distant fire was completely still once more.

Still, but watchful.

It seemed the very earth was waiting for its

pulsing hungry consummation, ready to assume form and identity when the moment was ripe. In a shroud of expanding creeping shapes, dead things stirred through a billowing cloud of seeping mist. There was nothing tangible, but the whole wood vibrated with a strange new life of its own. And on the fringe of festivities the unknown stranger watched.

Watched and waited.

For it was Samain.

CHAPTER TWELVE

The fire was bright in the clearing when the antlered, massive figure of Manfred Hearne strode through the trees. All the expected participants of the event were already present, and on the far side of the little group Adam watched steadily as Manfred with a tremendous show of geniality took a central position, lifting an arm in a gesture of welcome.

'Glad to see you, friends,' he said in clear booming tones. 'On such a night, at such a time, we can all now experience the living ancient truth of Mag-Mell, and of the risen dead—' his voice went on, while Yvonne like a disorientated fragile giant moth in her beads and draperies flitted to and fro with dishes and plates.

Bran, on the fringe of the site, was pouring the wine, and handing each a glass, moving with the strange impersonality of one who'd performed the role countless times before. Yet his eyes as he came towards Lucinda showed a brief interest and speculation that stirred a mounting awareness in her. Adam flung her a quick glance; but her pose was static and controlled, almost too rigid to be natural. Then, lifting an arm, she took the proffered wine. Bran's head was slightly inclined towards her. She was about to drink when Adam's hand closed quickly on her wrist, forcing the glass downwards so the wine spilled in a golden trickle on the ground.

'What are you doing?' she whispered furiously. 'What's the matter with you?'

Adam said nothing. His eyes were hard, his mouth a tight line of censure.

Aleyne shivered. She appeared to accept her own portion, but made a pretence merely of drinking. Manfred, who was still continuing his oration, allowed his eyes to slip furtively in her direction, lingering with anticipatory momentary pleasure on her slim form and pale hair washed to molten gold by the leaping flames. Against her will she felt a part of herself intimidated by their hypnotic power. In the short interim before she could force herself to look away she had a strange impression of countless beings and ages reborn from spheres far beyond the limits of time—pictures that came and went like those resurrected on a screen, yet uncannily alive. The red of the fire licked the narrowed orbs to an ever-changing flickering crimson. Their message was clear. 'I will have you. You are mine.'

With mounting sickness spreading through her senses, she felt her shiver deepen and become a drawn-out shudder. Her head drooped.

She felt Adam's hand touch hers.

'Aleyne—what is it? Are you ill?'

She made a gesture of denial, and looked up at him. 'Don't leave me,' she said.

The pressure of his hand increased. 'Like hell I won't,' he whispered. She relaxed a little and when she'd recovered she became aware that Hearne was concluding his speech of welcome and announcing the opening of proceedings.

'First of all,' he said, 'the living proof of Mag-Mell and Tir-Na-Noc will be displayed by an introductory item by one of our most devoted members, Yvonne Court, who is prepared to present herself as a legendary symbol of youth eternal.'

There was a pause.

Then he said with an arm outspread— 'Yvonne, my dear—your entrance.'

Across the patch of ground his antlered shadow zig-zagged fitfully from the curdling rosy light. And into that shadow suddenly danced another more macabre and witch-like,

155

the lean bedraggled-looking form of Yvonne Court.

Her thin arms were waving over her straggling locks, and through side-slits in her green dress bony legs were jerking and gyrating like those of a marionette. Her neck was bobbing from side to side, her wide mouth extended across her lean face in a senile grin.

It was horrible, uncanny, but *real*.

Aleyne hid her face on Adam's shoulder; Lucinda merely sat with a contemptuous sneer on her lovely lips. But her glance slid every few moments towards Bran, who was standing in the shadow of a tree. Seen from such an angle he seemed to have matured and grown. On his bright black curls the firelight danced, touching them to ruby-red. His eyes were warm for Lucinda, and she knew it.

Everyone else seemed hypnotised by the spectacle enacted for their benefit. By then the macabre scene was compelling—the grey mist oozing from the earth crept insidiously unnoticed towards them—billowing, writhing, twisting and groping upwards as though the demons of hell had been called upon to celebrate.

Hypnotised, half-shamed by the scene, the small crowd of watchers stood in a semi-circle, staring. Except for occasional half-whispered comments and sighs no one moved except with an instinctive groping from one hand to another, for human contact. And alone facing them from the other side, the massive figure of Hearne was outlined as a towering pagan entity, the dark god of his underlings.

Poppy was the first to feel the gradual stirring of human emotion and terror. As her heart began to pound against her chest and ears, her fingers closed involuntarily on Lloyd's wrist. 'Get me out of here—' she whispered. 'Lloyd—Lloyd—' but it was as though he was deaf to everything but the slow waking rhythm of the earth's deep heart.

As the gyrating wraith-like forms assumed more strength and positive identity, the eerie tones of Manfred's concerto rose fitfully at first, on a creeping breath of wind that shuddered and swelled through the night air, taking all and everyone apparently into its macabre unification.

Aleyne, with her eyes closed, let her head fall against Adam's shoulder. 'Save me, Adam,' she tried to say—'save me—' but no words came from her pale lips; and through her fallen lids the fiery glow of Manfred's eyes bored and claimed her. There was no darkness or peace for her; nothing but the image of his immense antlered head against the fire-lit shadows. On Adam's other side Lucinda never moved. Her form was completely static, her eyes glazed. Peering from the clustered tree trunks behind Hearne, Bran's glance burned and held her. Everywhere there were eyes— eyes of a thousand risen unseen beings—with

157

those of Rose, Hiram, Emily, Freddie, Poppy and Lloyd.

And Adam.

Adam whose sense and will were stretched to breaking point, but whose mind was clear.

Time died.

Most of those present had automatically taken Manfred's unholy brew. But Adam's glass, with Aleyne's, lay empty by his side; the other was smashed by a stone. Darkness and light became fused into one, a swirling vortex of blackness and flame through which the wild twirling form of Yvonne Court was fitfully glimpsed, then lost again. From beyond the wood came a sudden hurricane of creaking, cracking sound, followed by shrill high screaming, and a vast shadow filling the sky as though some malevolent giant bird for a second blotted out the universe.

Rose doubled up and, but for Hiram's arm supporting her, would have fallen to the ground.

Yvonne's macabre form suddenly crumpled and lay, clawing the air at Hearne's foot. A boot came out and gave her a contemptuous push. There was no pity or compassion or shred of human warmth anymore—not even desire on Manfred's flame-lit face. Only lust.

Lust for Aleyne.

Aleyne sensed it and understood. Her whole body was a shudder of terror, even with Adam's hand tightly enclosed on her wrist. He pushed something into her hand. She gripped it half-consciously and held it to her breast.

Manfred moved purposefully, slowly, towards them, his lips twisted into a smile of curious malignancy.

'And now—' he whispered on the wind's breath, 'what about a game—a game of hide-and-seek—the game of children, the children of Mag-Mell?'

There was silence for a moment, and then a sudden scuffling as figures pushed this way and that; to hide? Or to escape? None had time or means to answer. The misted earth heaved and coiled and stretched for succour—the succour of Man. Hearne's eyes burned more brightly than any mortal flame. But Adam's were cold; colder than the hardest ice.

Confrontation was stealthy in its approach. But Lucinda did not see. All she was aware of was Bran's dark form suddenly clarified and clear against the trees. He stood apart, watching and calling, though his voice was no more than an echo of the wind's sigh. But in it for her was all beauty and the reason for which she had been born. Recognition, beyond the barriers of age and time, flowered between them. With her arms outstretched she went rushing towards him.

The rest fell away.

As his slant eyes claimed her, he was no longer half-child, half-youth, but tall in his manhood towering above her; a young god born of the timeless regions, resurrected beyond all limitations of the flesh.

Hand in hand they wandered deep into the wood. The trees were hushed and closed about them. Except for a faint lingering drift of light tipping his dark curls and a half-lingering rosy sheen on her pale face, all was dark. No stars, no ray of the climbing moon filtered the branches. No glimmering path to point the way.

But they knew.

Destiny stronger than their own selves, more compelling than reason, mortal knowledge or any span of human years, flowered from the unknown abyss, glorifying their coming together in the magic hinterland of Mag-Mell.

Very gently he laid her down on the soft earth. Her eyes were wide with wonder when she looked up and saw his face which was no longer entirely Bran's—but of the dark stranger's—staring down on her. Slowly her arms went out and her body lurched to receive him. In the moment before giving and taking, of consummation through complete union, Lucinda knew with a brief stab of clarity she was surrendering all, as he too was—that they were both the sacrifice of that night-out-of-time, which at the first glow of dawn would be erased forever.

From the distance the sound of eerie music rustled and whined on the winter air. There was a shudder of the earth's surface. A cry from Lucinda of anguish and appeasement as her body jerked once, convulsively, and was still.

The last thing she saw was his face—the face of the stranger—burning with a fleeting brightness that absorbed for her the whole world.

Then, his own young flesh changed, gradually withered, becoming sunken and dry with age.

There was a cackling high crescendo of malicious laughter, the crackle of twigs and a shudder when he fell.

After that, silence complete and absolute.

*   *   *

It was not until morning that Lucinda's body was found. She was lying on her back quite dead, with her eyes cold and glazed, facing the sky.

Beside her lay the withered brown body of a very very ancient man, so old he could almost have been a mummy. No one had seen him before; no one knew from where he'd come.

Bran would have been able to tell them.

But Bran had disappeared.

CHAPTER THIRTEEN

Aleyne, afterwards, remembered nothing of the macabre events, following Lucinda's unnoticed escape into the trees with Bran, and Adam did not tell her. All he wished himself was to forget, though he doubted he ever would. Whatever normal life he might salvage for any future with Aleyne, the memory of Samain would never completely be erased from his mind—of Manfred's immense form approaching stealthily towards them, licked to lurid flames from the fire—of the three grotesque screaming figures leaping in immense bat-like shapes round the prone body of Yvonne who lay stark and writhing on a spot of charred ground.

No nightmare dreamed by man could have held such incredible horror and abomination; no evil of the Black Arts have rivalled the satanic deadly power of the vile lust in Hearne's narrowed eyes as a great hand emerged, fingers extended, tracing curious signs on the thickened air. Adam, frozen to static immobility, had felt Aleyne slump in a dead weight against his chest, with one arm supporting her; the other, after the paralysed interim, had managed somehow to locate the little cross he'd given her and thrust it forward. Strange ancient incantations in a language he'd never known broke from his lips. Manfred had lurched forward, over the vile swarming ground, where evil squirmed and squealed before slowly disintegrating into grey air. Then, with arms extended, his great body had suddenly toppled backwards and fallen. His mouth was open, and it had seemed to Adam that fork-tongued serpents rose from the gaping jaws before withering into nothing.

The dark trees had appeared to retreat a little from the shocked gathering of human beings. There was a shaking and sighing of the whole terrain—a rising whistling of wind carrying three black shapes high above into the moon-washed sky; a wail and scream of a feline form as it swooped through the shadows to land on Hearne's large breast, wild slit eyes dazed and staring, mouth extended malignantly from ear to ear.

Then all was silent except for the mad laughter of a crazy giant with antlered crown jutting starkly from the ground. The huddled crowd of human beings had not moved for a minute, then shocked to mobility they had suddenly turned and blundered lumberingly as though woken from a drunken sleep, towards the wood's edge.

Adam had looked round for Lucinda, and not finding her had proceeded after the others with Aleyne in his arms.

For a long time afterwards he was to blame himself, and wonder; wonder if through greater effort on his part he might have saved his wife.

But when she was found the next day he realised that this would not have been her wish. Her face in death was ecstatic; her looks etherealised into something more than mere mortal beauty. Whether right or wrong, Lucinda obviously had found her Mag-Mell and Tir-Na-Noc.

This was the only vindicating factor of the whole event.

*   *   *

For a time following the unwholesome event and police enquiries concerning the deaths of Lucinda and Yvonne, a curious silence overhung the district of Summerhayes. Efforts were made by everyone concerned to keep details from the press. But Black Magic rituals entailing the unexplainable demise of two human beings, and a third, Manfred Hearne, being forcibly ushered to a home for the insane, was hardly the type of news to escape avid journalists, and the Sunday papers, in particular, made lurid money's worth out of it.

'I don't like it, Hiram,' Rose said, with a shudder of nerves. 'Seeing it all in print makes it all the worse somehow. And that bit about the boy—Bran? They think he could've been murdered and buried somewhere in the wood. Listen to this—"it is still thought the boy may have met his death by fair means or foul, and his body interned nearby. Full police enquiries

164

and investigations are in progress and the woodland and moors being thoroughly combed! The identity of the old man discovered by the dead woman has not yet been solved."'

'Hm,' Hiram said thoughtfully, 'and it's my guess it never will be.'

'What do you mean, Hiram? Why do you say that?'

Her husband paused before replying. Then he said, 'A lot of funny things happened that night, love, unhealthy wicked things too. What we imagined and what was true is a kind of a mystery, if you ask me. Best not to delve too much. Try and forget what you can of it, and avoid the papers. Then when the police've finished poking and probing, we'll be out in no time and say goodbye to this place for good.'

Rose was silent before saying, 'I can hardly bear to wait for it. Funny, isn't it? Now everything's over—the bad things I mean— we've got to get rid of a real nice home. I suppose it *does* make sense? But not when you think about it in a normal way. Do you see what I mean?'

'Guess I do, love. Common sense. But the common sense isn't always what it seems. If you think too hard about what's what, you can get into a muddle of thought; and it's not good for ordinary folk like you and me. People— that's what we need, crowds and streets and a bit of gossip when we feel like it. You especially. Remember how you enjoyed your weekly shopping jaunts at the stores and those select places in the West End? Why—you haven't had a new hat in months. Not a single bargain or high-spending spree, and that's unnatural for your kind of woman.'

Rose smiled fondly.

'How right you are, Hiram. As you say—it's best not to go too deep into things. But I'd never have thought it—that the simple life could be such a—such a complicated frightening business.'

So the matter, for the Saunders, was settled.

With Poppy and Lloyd it was a little different.

'Why should we sell?' Poppy said defensively. 'I've spent a lot on this house. It's artistic, it's got style. And it's—well an advertisement in a way.'

'For what? Your belated stage blossoming?'

Poppy flushed. 'You needn't sneer.'

He noticed that one hand was twisting a handkerchief into a small tight ball, and guessed that she was more overwrought than she pretended to be, and might even be accepting life there as a challenge—a boost to her own bravery and self-esteem.

His arm slipped round her waist.

'Come on now. I'm not sneering. And I know what you mean about style and all the rest. But I don't want a broody chick for a wife. Get me? I know you've got guts to stick any

166

bad memories lingering about. And I'd back you against a ghost any day. But the time's come to take the armour off, Poppy. This district's too off-beat and peculiar for my taste, and *I* should know.'

'With you I wouldn't be afraid—not of anything,' Poppy told him, the strain fading from her eyes to dewy softness.

'O.K. Then all you have to do is what I say,' he retorted firmly. '*I'm* leaving, and if you're so dead set on your new husband's company as you make out, you'll come with me.'

There was a pause before he added, 'Understand?'

'Yes, Lloyd,' Poppy agreed equably. 'Perhaps you're right.'

Under other circumstances she would probably have made a more determined effort to have her own way. But with the lingering macabre memory of past events still rising at odd moments to chill her mind, she was basically relieved to accept Lloyd's decision.

Emily Carson had to accept no one's.

A fortnight following Samain and the opening of police investigations, Freddie had taken himself off to his paramour in Penzance, informing his wife with heartless candour that he was sick of her and her high-faluting friends, her apron strings and money-bags and was off to a new life.

'And don't make out you're surprised,' he said, as a parting shock. 'You know how you

167

got me, and what I married you for. Well, we had our moments at the beginning and when I shut my eyes I thought the good life made things worth it. But it's *not* been good, and to tell you the truth, Em, the idea of spending years and years ahead watching you grow stouter and meaner and sillier every day is enough to send anyone up the wall. Sorry. But there it is.'

A few minutes later, Emily, stony-eyed, had watched his slim insignificant figure swing down the front path and out of the gate with a bag in his hand, looking for all the world, she thought bitterly, like some complacent cocky little salesman who'd just accomplished some successful commercial deal.

At first the full implications didn't register. When they did she felt a dull rage spread through her cumbrous body, mounting in a crimson flood to her face. She could imagine the smug smile on his lips when he told his mistress of the final scene between them—bragging of his own powers and contemptuous dismissal of the dull elderly woman he'd married. The room seemed to swim round her sickeningly. Failure. All was failure—she'd been nothing in his life but a pawn and means to an end. He'd already enough in the bank by now to help set up a pleasant little menage for the two of them.

'*Devils, devils,*' a voice screamed through her inner ear, and as the whirring confusion in her head ebbed and flowed in a monstrous tide of despair, she reached out instinctively for support. Her fingers touched the edge of a small table, but it evaded full contact and fell crashing to the floor, followed a second later by the thud of her own form.

Her eyes opened for a moment, staring at the ceiling with glazed rigidity. Then, as her breath quickened, rising raspingly from her choking lungs, a shadow gathered intensity from a corner of the room, spreading menacingly towards her. For an interim of time that could have been minutes or longer, it hovered above, then took her into complete darkness.

Outside rain began to fall, beating with mournful persistence against the window. On a nearby branch a cat sat hunched against the elements, watching as though in vigil.

When all was over it slipped away into the shadows, prowling stealthily in the direction of Magswikk. Though his master, Hearne, was no longer at his cottage, there were still others of his kind about. Those who despite a padded cell had access and means of communication.

No one knew the cat's destination. No one saw; and it was not until the next day that Emily's body was found lying cold and helpless on her living room floor.

*　　　*　　　*

'Of course, it was a stroke,' Lloyd said when the news became known. 'Poor old Emily. But you know, she *did* have a raw deal from that bastard. Trouble was she couldn't accept the truth. Well—perhaps it's a good thing she's out of it.'

Poppy's lips twitched nervously. There was reproach in her voice when she said, 'I think that's rather a terrible thing to say, Lloyd. Not to be alive, or see or hear things—not to be here when the spring comes—' her voice wavered off uncertainly.

Lloyd grimaced and slid his arm round her waist reassuringly. 'Come on now, none of that. Think of *us*, and be damned grateful we're still about and kicking.'

'I am—I *am*,' Poppy insisted. 'That's just it. Every new day seems to bring another shock, and you never know—'

'Stop it. Shut up, darling,' Lloyd said, sharply, 'or you may find yourself landing up alone like Emily.'

'I'm sorry. I didn't mean to be morbid.'

'Maybe. But you bloody well *were*,' he reminded her. 'And that all goes to show I'm right in seeing we get away as soon as possible.'

'Yes. I know.'

'What about a drink?'

'No, thanks,' Poppy said surprisingly.

'Hm. Well, just as you like. Personally I've never felt more like a boost in my life.'

He crossed to the cabinet, poured a double

170

whisky and drank it. When he turned Poppy was still staring rather dejectedly towards the window.

'What's on your mind now?' he asked.

'I was wondering about Adam and Aleyne. You'd have thought *they*'d've been gone already. I mean with Lucinda dying like that—'

'Like what, for pete's sake? A heart attack—fright—and more than her share of Hearne's pernicious drug? There wasn't exactly anything suspicious about her death—materially speaking. You heard it all, the inquest was clear enough.'

'Yes. I know; but Lucinda *was* Adam's wife. I should have thought as thing's were with Aleyne and him he'd have wanted to be off as soon as possible.'

'Adam has his reasons, I guess,' Lloyd said curtly. 'So do you mind dropping the subject?'

'All right. But you needn't bark at me,' Poppy retorted with a rush of her old spirit.

Lloyd's reference to Adam was in fact precisely true. He *did* have his reasons, which Aleyne was well aware of, though he was curiously secretive over the matter. There had been a number of small patterns in Adam's behaviour since Lucinda's death that had puzzled her. His insistence for instance that Lucinda's body should be cremated at Truro miles away with no one present but himself, instead of laid to rest quietly in nearby Maggswikk churchyard.

171

But for some time, even before Samain he'd seemed oddly averse to visiting the village. And after his wife's death the feeling had intensified.

'They don't like us there,' he'd said once, 'and to tell the truth I'm not keen on the place myself. It might be better to do all the shopping in Penzance or some other centre, the same as Poppy and Lloyd.'

'All right,' Aleyne had agreed. 'Though I don't see—'

'Shsh—' his lips had come gently down upon her own. 'Trust me, my love. Try and understand. There are a few things I've got to work out here. I don't know how long it will take; a week or two maybe, then I'll explain, and we can leave Summerhayes as soon as we choose. Aleyne—?'

Her clear eyes stared into his unblinkingly and all the compassion in him went out to her. 'I love you, you know,' he said gently. 'Never, *never* forget that. And when this is over, after a reasonable time—'

'Yes?'

'You *will* marry me, won't you?'

'Of course,' she answered quietly. 'You should know that by now.' There was a pause, then she added, 'Is it because of the villagers you want to shun Magswikk, because of us being alone here now?'

He shook his head. 'I've no doubt tongues were wagging long before—Lucinda died,' he said with an effort. 'I just don't want you involved in anything else unpleasant—if there *is* anything.'

By the sudden withdrawal of his arm, a certain remote speculation in his voice and eyes, she knew he was certain there *was* something and her whole body and spirit were chilled again. Sometimes when she was alone she found herself stiffening, with a mild chattering of her teeth. She'd force herself to look out then towards the wood or from the back of the house to the sea. There was nothing unusual there—no creeping shadow, or rarely—to terrify her nerves. But the desolation at those times was overwhelming; if Adam was around she'd find him and following some brief conversation over a perfectly mundane matter he'd sense the tension in her and take her into his arms.

'Make love to me,' her heart would cry, 'please make me warm and live again.'

But he didn't. The desire in him, she knew, was there. But it was as though he was waiting until they could begin their real life together in a new atmosphere, with the dark puzzle of Magswikk solved and put behind them.

Poppy and Lloyd left the district at the end of February. The early spring had been mostly dull and dreary, with grey skies more often than not heralding rain. They had a brief goodbye party with Adam and Aleyne the night before, which was more of a strain than a pleasure. Lloyd, particularly, was not forthcoming about their reasons for going, not wishing to admit fear of atmosphere. He was over-cheerful, drank too much, and Poppy's manner was far too affectionate to be genuine, put on, obviously to hide strain.

'You two darlings must come up for a week as soon as you can,' she told them gushingly. 'We'll really feel quite *lost* without you about. It's been such fun—in a way—' her voice trailed away half wistfully, then continued with forced brightness, 'but you know how it is—the country life's okay for a time, and *you* fit in better somehow. Lloyd and me though—I'm afraid we're rather sophisticated. Not half so—self-sufficient as you. I admire you terrifically.'

'For heaven's sake, Poppy, spare the gab,' Lloyd said rudely. 'If you're still so dead set on making a stage come-back you'd better start getting things in proportion.'

Poppy flushed.

'He's a rude man, isn't he, Aleyne?' she said. 'But then—' smiling tartly, though with a sharp glance at her husband, 'I always knew that. I used to find it quite intriguing, until I married him.'

Lloyd's eyes narrowed. 'You mean until *I* married you, my dear,' he said promptly.

'Yes, of course.'

The evening ended eventually on a note of discomforted regret, although the regret, Adam and Aleyne both knew was mostly

174

assumed.

The following morning they both stood at the door of Summerhayes to wave as the car carried Poppy and Lloyd away.

'So that's that,' Adam said, as he led Aleyne back into the house. 'Now we're well and truly alone.'

'*Are* we?' Aleyne asked quietly but meaningfully.

He glanced at her quickly. In the early morning light her face was briefly shadowed as though a phantom hand had brushed it, and when his eyes instinctively strayed to the floor he saw a strange zig-zag shape cross it, moving fitfully up the wall where it unpredictably faded.

A curtain drifting from the wind perhaps? Or a cloud passing the watery sunlight? But there were no curtains by the door, and there was no wind to waft any cloud away. He gripped Aleyne's hand tightly. 'What do you mean, *are* we? Of course we are.'

'I suppose so,' she said. 'I mustn't go imagining things but don't try to put me off either, Adam. If I stay, we must share things, mustn't we?'

'If? Yes, that's what I've been wondering.'

'What do you mean?' He waited before suggesting, 'Perhaps you ought to leave, darling. God knows, I don't want you to. But it wouldn't be for long, and if your peace of mind was assured—'

175

'No.' Her voice was very definite. 'While you need me, Adam—or want me—I'm staying. As a matter of fact I'm staying anyway. You see, I'm just as puzzled as you about—'

'Yes?'

'The identity of that wizened old man. The one lying near—Lucinda,' she said significantly. 'That *is* why you're staying, isn't it?'

'Partly.'

'Partly?'

'Only partly,' he told her. 'And I very much doubt we shall get far there.'

'Then—?'

'Sh—sh,' he put a finger gently on her lips before kissing her. 'Leave it at that for the present. In time—you shall be in on everything. I promise.'

She smiled wrily. 'I wonder. You're over-protective of me, you know. It isn't as if I hadn't—hadn't—'

'What?'

'Experienced frightening things already. That night at Beltane, remember? There was the stranger, or prowler as you like to call him. And then the ridiculous way I was besotted by Manfred's tune—'

'That's *one* thing you won't be troubled by again,' Adam said grimly. 'Hearne's well and truly off the map now.'

'So you say,' she remarked quietly.

'Yes, I *do*.' Both arms gripped her shoulders

176

firmly. 'And you must believe it, understand?'

'Oh yes,' she answered mechanically, adding a moment later with simulated assurance, 'I know you're right, Adam.'

'Good.'

But she didn't know. There were times when she fancied an echo of the insidious melody still stirred and rustled through the branches of the trees outside—moments when she half fancied she saw a large shadowed shape watching from across the lane. Then, when she'd brushed a hand across her eyes it had gone, and there was no sound anymore but those of nature—creaking of bushes and thin moaning of wind round the house.

'Spring is nearly here,' she'd tell herself, 'soon the primroses will be properly out and bluebells growing in the wood.'

But she doubted in her secret self that flowers would ever star that certain piece of terrain again. Though she hid the fact from Adam she couldn't erase the picture from her mind of Lucinda lying on the cold earth and Yvonne crumpled up like a broken scarecrow in the clearing.

She wondered more frequently why Adam was so insistent on her not going to Magswikk. Once, when she thought he was working upstairs she went out with a vague intention of going that way, and was surprised to meet him round the bend coming from the direction of the village.

She got a quick remark in before he could say anything.

'I *thought* so.' (Liar) 'Doing the very thing you're determined I shouldn't.'

He slipped his arm round her waist, and gave a short laugh. But his eyes were worried when he said, 'Don't pretend, Aleyne: I know you too well. You took the first chance of slipping off when I was out of the way. Please don't—not up there.'

'Very well. You have my promise.'

They walked back to the house silently. She would have broken the barrier if she could, but there seemed nothing to say. It occurred to her with a pang that Lucinda, who had been her half-sister and Adam's wife, had been rather easily eradicated from any topic of conversation they had together and when back in the kitchen at Summerhayes Aleyne said suddenly, 'Don't you miss her at all, Adam— Lucinda, I mean.'

He stared at her for a moment, then replied, 'Of course I miss her. So do you. Lucinda wasn't the type of woman to be written off without leaving a bit of a blank space now and again, and sometimes I feel I was unfair. But there's no point in dwelling on facts like that. I didn't want her to die, but she did. And I have you. For that I thank God.'

'Yes. And I think God is very much needed round here,' Aleyne told him. 'Not only here. Perhaps everywhere. Life's pretty selfish when you think about it, isn't it? We *want* things and go all out after them, and then—' she shivered slightly.

He shook his head slowly. 'My dear love— *you* can't be accused of doing that. In a way that's a pity. As I've said before, if you'd used *your* claws more, the whole sad business of my marriage to Lucinda could have been avoided. I guess men are weaker than women in one respect—apt to grab any tit-bit under their noses—provided it's juicy enough. And instead of fighting you just walked off and left me to it. Pride I suppose you'd call it, but I'd give it another name. Sheer idiocy.'

Aleyne recalled Lucinda herself saying almost the same thing, and made no comment, although she felt, wrily, that Adam, like most men, had a particular capacity of putting the blame at anyone's door but his own.

March passed into early April, with grey days gradually giving way to sunsplashed mornings interspersed occasionally with showers of thin rain. A few celandines and primroses starred the ditches and woodlands, but the earth round there, generally, seemed dull and tired, and disinclined to blossom. It was as though life had been drained from it, Aleyne thought frequently, and the joy of springtime damned by Samain. Few small wild creatures disturbed the slowly thrusting bracken; the chatter of birds was seldom heard. The cottages round Summerhayes stood bereft, with bleak empty eyes turned to the lanes. At intervals house agents brought prospective purchasers to inspect properties. But after the first visit the same people never returned. Loneliness encompassed the landscape; even the help who came to Summerhayes from a nearby farm grew daily more sullen and disinclined to talk.

'You haven't much to say for yourself these days,' Aleyne told her once. 'Is anything worrying you, Mrs Clay?'

The woman, who was middle-aged, dumpy and pale, with a wary glint in her dark eyes, answered a trifle belligerently, 'Not more than usual. I don't see what makes you ask, mum. I do my work proper, doan'I?'

'Oh yes, yes, of course,' Aleyne answered hurriedly. 'I wasn't complaining. Please don't think that. Only—it *does* seem very quiet round here sometimes.'

'Folks who doan' like quiet shouldn' tek land here then,' came the answer promptly. 'Everything was all right till all them furriners came pokin' 'bout.'

'Including me, I suppose,' Aleyne said.

'I wasn' referrin' to you, mum,' Mrs Clay answered with a lift of her plump chin. 'I'm not the kind to work for pay an' go criticize them who gives the money.' Her tones held an affront.

'Oh no, I'm sure. I didn't mean that,' Aleyne tried to assure her helplessly. 'Please don't get me wrong. I—'

'I don't think I do, mum—*Miss*,' the woman said, with a significant emphasis on the last word. 'I know my place, and I know since the lady of the house died, pore thing, you have taken over just where she left off. Some things doan' need explaining, and ef you doan' mind I prefer not to talk about them.'

'I *do* mind, I'm afraid,' Aleyne retorted sharply. 'You're suggesting things that aren't true. There is nothing—nothing improper about my relationship to Mr Fayne. So I'd be grateful if you put such an idea out of your head immediately.'

The moment she'd spoken, Aleyne could have bitten her tongue out for resorting to such an undignified argument.

Mrs Clay threw her a sharp glance, 'I didn' say anythin' like that,' she retorted snappily. 'But now you've brought it up I may as well tell you, mum, that I've bin thinkin' for some time yet would be better I stopped workin' here. Magswikk folk've bin' talkin' an' you can't blame them. Oh, I'm not the one to listen to idle gossip. To keep my mind shut to what doan' concern me, 'as always bin my way. But the fact is now spring's here I'm needed more at the farm, so I'd be obliged if you'd take my notice as from a week today.' Aleyne was temporarily stunned.

'But a moment ago you said everything was all right—'

'What I said was, I knew my *place* and that's quite different,' Mrs Clay snapped. 'All *right*?' She gave a short laugh, more of a bark. 'I'm sure, mum, you know very well that it edn? *Nothing's* right 'bout this place, an' ef I was you I'd get out sharp, same as I'll be doin' in a week's time!'

She turned, left the room abruptly, and in sudden panic Aleyne knew she'd meant what she'd said. The extra work entailed with the woman's departure would not bother her but the contemplation of being alone in the house whenever Adam happened to be out searching libraries for books or for some jaunt on his own business in Penzance or Penjust, filled Aleyne with momentary terror.

Reason told her there was nothing to be afraid of, but then reason so far had had little to do with happenings round Summerhayes and Magswikk. At such times as this she wondered if she should have agreed with Adam's earlier suggestion for her to leave. Then, when her nerves settled into some sort of perspective, she was determined that whatever happened she'd stay, and somehow keep her fears to herself. Adam meanwhile proceeded with his historical delvings into the area's past, making as well concentrated studies of the indigenous qualities of the surrounding district. Like Aleyne he'd noticed the parched appearance of the earth following the tragedies of Samain—almost as though any

182

substance it had held, had been drained away.

Once when he was stirring a piece of ground on the fringe of the wood with a stick, a farm labourer came up to him and said, 'Not good land round eer, surr. They shud cut et all down an' plough up, or else burn et.'

'Why burn?'

'Purifyin, that's what I do mean,' the man said. 'I've worked land all my life, an' whether you believe et or not, there's some all rich an' ready to yield good growth, as God meant, an' some that's thrivin' with devil's seed, like this eer.'

'And above? Over there beyond the turn?' Adam questioned, pointing in the direction of the hummock of ground where the ancient elders stood.

The man turned his head slowly.

'Ah. To the left you do mean.'

'Yes.'

'Keep away. Steer clear of et,' the man told Adam. 'No one with any sense goes there anymore. Not that I'm the sort to be scared of three wicked old besoms who died at the stake. But there's other things; things that bring a darkness to the soul. An' doan' you say I'm imagining. When you live close to nature you learn things no others would dream 'bout.' He paused, then added, 'I'll be on my way. Sorry ef I've brought gloom on 'ee. Good day, surr.'

'Good day,' Adam replied mechanically.

A darkness of the soul, he thought when the

183

man had gone, what an apt description for the spreading yet unseen forces encompassing the vicinity.

He recalled his unproductive visit to Magswikk vicarage where he'd encountered the unhelpful and unsavoury dumpy clergyman with his hypocritical regrets and probing secretive eyes. If he'd wanted he could have provided the information Adam asked for. But for some reason—and *'dark'* was the only adjective applicable, he'd been as off-putting as possible.

Why?

Had he been in some way involved with the evil rites of Samain? Known more of Hearne than he professed? Such things had happened in the past. There was the instance quoted in the old library book concerning the rector Silas Carnverrych who had lusted after Mercy, one of the witches hanged in 1698, and after being repulsed he'd given evidence against her. Was it possible that tainted atmosphere could linger and poison the very characters moving within its orbit? If so, then how unfortunate for the inhabitants of the village.

He tried to dispel the idea as a mere side issue and unimportant. But the thought still lingered persistently at the back of his mind, and he decided that on the first opportunity he'd make a return visit, on the flimsy pretext of informing the cleric that he'd managed to obtain a book on the subject he'd required and was therefore sorry he'd bothered him over the matter in the first place. No doubt he'd be greeted with a rebuff, perhaps open hostility and a tirade of blame for the terrible results of the pagan feast. The area round Summerhayes must have become an unforgettable scandal and one which would never be erased. The rector would not be the only one to condemn. There might even be stone-throwing if his—Adam's—presence was suspected. Therefore he'd take the car out one morning early before many villagers were about, and have his confrontation at the rectory as man to man.

Or was that the term to use?

Adam smiled sardonically to himself. Hardly. There were, he thought, in the words of the Bard—more things in heaven and earth than are dreamed of in our philosophy.

He said nothing of his intention to Aleyne until the evening before. They had just finished tea, and were standing at the window of the sitting room watching a flame of winter sunset beyond the trees to the west. His arm was round her, her head resting on his shoulder.

'Strange, isn't it?' she said softly. 'Nature can be so lovely sometimes, and at others so—horrible.'

'Nature's not horrible,' Adam said. 'It's only the *un*natural that causes havoc and disorientation—*spiritual* disorientation.'

'I suppose so,' she remarked doubtfully.

His hand tightened on her waist, then he

said, 'Aleyne, I'd like you to take off somewhere tomorrow, just for the morning. I'll drive you to the nearest bus stop, or all the way if you like, and meet you on the twelve-thirty back.'

She glanced at him in astonishment. '*Why*, Adam? What's the reason for wanting me out of the way.'

'I'm going to Magswikk,' he told her, 'to see that odious little rector I told you about. It may be an unpleasant interview, but it's something I have to do.'

'Something to do with Samain?'

'Yes. And I don't want you within ear or eye-shot.'

'But—' her voice was doubtful. 'Why on earth can't I stay here?'

His hand brushed her head lightly.

'In the first place, my love, you'd probably get an attack of the horrors—you've had enough cause lately in all conscience. In the second I want to be sure you're safely out of reach of any possible vendetta, spiritual or otherwise, so my mind is free to get down to things in my own way. Got it?'

She shook her head. 'No. But then I haven't a clue at the moment what exactly's in your head.'

'And that's as it should be,' he replied. 'Anyway—a bit of a shopping spree will do you good. There must be a few things you want, personal bits and pieces—'

186

'Oh yes,' she forced herself to say brightly. 'Don't worry, Adam, I can take a hint. You don't need to tell me my hair's a mess and my hands need a manicure, my skin needs beautifying and that it will be a relief to see a new up-dated Aleyne walk in afterwards.'

'Don't you dare change yourself one bit,' he said quickly. 'If you do—'

'Well?'

'Wait and see,' he said, kissing her.

So the matter was left there, and the following day shortly after breakfast, Adam drove Aleyne into Penzance, and after a brief break for coffee in a popular arty-crafty cafe, started back again for Summerhayes and Magswikk.

The morning was grey but clear, with the landscape silhouetted starkly under the sky. Everything appeared as though newly washed from rain; but the very clarity, somehow, seemed highly-charged with menace and unease. Birds flew dark over the hedges and tree-tops; in the distance to the right, the sea held a glassy brightness that was hard against the horizon.

As he drove along Adam's thoughts wandered back instinctively to past events and Lucinda. Guilt gnawed at him that he'd not missed her more, and that he couldn't now look back on her with warmth or love. Was that another of Hearne's insidious tricks—to have dwarfed human emotions to such meagre proportions? Adam had a shrewd inkling that Manfred had had all he wanted of Lucinda. At the time he'd resented it with a stab of primitive jealousy that had as quickly died. Now he didn't care at all—except with regret for her, and the shock she must have suffered when she realised the truth about the man.

The expression on her dead face though—so serene and softened, what had caused it? And who on earth was the ancient withered old man lying beside her? He doubted the police or anyone else would ever solve the macabre riddle, or the boy Bran's disappearance unless it was Hearne himself: and from what he'd heard very little hope was given that Manfred would recover sufficient sanity to express a coherent opinion on anything.

As he swung round the turn giving a view of the three elms, he had the curious sensation of a shadowed antlered shape standing by a huddle of hedgerow. Instinctively he looked away, but for a moment a frightening darkness crossed his eyes. His senses stiffened, giving rigidity to his spine and muscles of the neck. A second later it was over, and he saw with relief, the village in the dip below. He drove on slowly, drew into a gap in the hedge where a track led to a farm gate, parked the car there, got out and turned his head towards the hummock of ground where the church and vicarage stood. There was nothing in any way abnormal about the appearance of the former which had a characteristic air about it of being custodian of many centuries of memorials and past lives.

But the house was different.

Something had changed about it, Adam thought, since his last visit. He stood staring at it, and lit a cigarette before making any move to the gate of the narrow drive. The square face of the building seemed to have deteriorated curiously. The windows appeared strangely blank and uncurtained, like dead eyes watching—though 'dead' was hardly an apt word to use. Before forcing himself to go ahead Adam was certain he saw movement behind the glass, the suggestion of a dark shape, followed by a fleeting swimming disc of a face that the next moment was gone. It could have been the rector, or more likely a trick of light caused by sun or a waft of wind, he decided.

That though was impossible, he told himself the next moment.

There was no wind.

And no sun.

Nothing but the grey still day, and the grey granite building standing cold and forbidding under the chill sky.

And the 'thing' inside.

Why he suddenly began to think of a 'thing' instead of a human being was impossible to say. But as he walked down the path Adam, with increasing dread in him, was convinced no good influence waited to receive him. He realised too that what he'd imagined when he got out of the car was true. The house *was* different from what it had been on his earlier visit. One of the front windows had glass broken from a pane; the walls were crumbled, with a few stones littered by the sparse grass. The paint-work was peeled, and the door knocker fallen from its hinges.

Adam stood briefly, staring.

What did it mean? Had the occupant suddenly taken off and before doing so created just as much destruction as he could? Or was the whole thing a mirage? Some ghastly aberration of his own—Adam's—mind?

He left the porch and went to a window, clearing what glass there was, with a hand. His eyes could hardly accept what he saw—no furniture, except a tumbled ancient chair with rotted legs strewn about the floor; no carpet or covering on the flagstones, no picture on the wall or sign of human habitation. Damp trickled everywhere. The place could have been in such a state for centuries.

As he stared, a lean shape like that of a rat scuttled from one corner of the room to another. There was a creaking in the distance. The door at the far end opened just a little and with frozen nerves Adam saw a pale moon-shaped face poke round, above a clerical collar. A second afterwards it had gone.

Adam darted from the window back to the

porch. He saw that the rotted woodwork was slightly ajar and with an effort he pushed the front door open sufficiently to force his way through.

The sound whined and scraped across the hall. His own footsteps made a hollow impact as though disturbing the realms of the dead. At the far end of the passage the shadows curdled and massed into a black shape. A beam of light like the wan flame of a candle flickered momentarily across a vaporous countenance regarding him from narrowed slit eyes. There was a half smile on the lecherous lips. The whole effect was incredibly evil. Yet Adam knew confrontation was inevitable.

He steeled himself to walk on, following the form as it turned and was taken into deeper darkness ahead.

The air was cold; *very* cold. As he groped half blindly down the corridor, both arms pushing at the dank air, Adam was aware of the thick brush of cob-webs on his face. Occasionally there was the scurry of animal patter and the red glare of eyes through the greyness. His feet slipped more than once, and he nearly fell on the squashed dampness of dead leaves. Eventually—how long he never knew—he reached a room that had presumably once been a kitchen, leading into a smaller one. The air there had a foul smell about it, although a chink of light penetrated a gap from a further door.

The shadowed figure seemed to thin and became elongated as it passed through.

Adam followed.

Immediately the waft of air, though unhealthily damp still, penetrated his lungs, warding off the wave of faintness that had threatened to swamp him. He paused a second to steady his legs, and looking ahead saw the black shape spiral momentarily, then settle once more into the squat malignant form he'd first seen. There was a narrow pathway leading between leafless bushes where the figure glided now, glancing back intermittently with a shudder of greenish light catching the half-turned moon face. At certain points it seemed to hurry as though wishing for oblivion. Although Adam was revolted at the thought of any contact, instinct was stronger, and he pressed on relentlessly, his clothes clinging to his spine with heavy sweat.

Near the end of the garden, or travesty of one, since everything reeked of deadness, decay and neglect, the flagstones were broken and oozing with rivulets of water intermingled with black earth. A broken fence bordered the strip of land, and it was there that the odious emanation suddenly stopped, thickened, and seemed to take on more substance. Two arms went up, gyrating in the grey air, as Hearne's had done at Samain; then through the silence there was a thin high pitched scream, a shiver of the earth, followed by—nothing.

Adam felt his legs and feet frozen to the ground. Not a muscle of his body moved. He felt empty, drained—a negative shell, with all impetus and warm blood in him chilled to ice. Through his cold mind he searched desperately for comfort and sustenance— something to break the vile spell of evil that had him defenceless in its grip. A prayer, like a gentle light, seemed to penetrate the darkness, and he found his lips whispering its appeal to God.

Mobility gradually returned to his limbs. He could feel the circulation spreading in a tide of life through him. He took a step or two forward and forced his eyes to the broken stone where the figure had disappeared. He touched it with the toe of his shoe. A trickle of dankness oozed through the crack.

Impelled by the instinctive knowledge he must somehow locate what was beneath, he knelt down and forced his hands under the flag. He tried to lift it, stubbing his fingers uselessly in the effort. Then he saw a broken spade lying a few yards away. It was rusted and must have been there for years, but the blade was practically intact. He gripped it hard and with both hands near the metal in case the rotted wood broke, he managed after several efforts to heave a portion of the stone up.

There was nothing in any way extraordinary to be seen at first—just the sodden earth and a few blackish pebbles lying embedded in

193

moisture. An insect or two darted about, and he noticed with revulsion a worm squirming where the blade had struck. Automatically he knelt down and started scrabbling again at the ground. The earth flew up in his face. He had a compulsive sensation that if he worked hard enough the conclusive secret of Samain and haunting of Summerhayes were about to be disclosed. So he continued relentlessly and unceasingly and presently he knew he was right.

A rusted tin box jutted from a hollow near a piece of buried granite. It could have been of any age; but an aura of evil emanated from its surface in a rush of foul smelling dust. Holding his breath for half a minute Adam unearthed it and laid it flat on the yellowish grass bordering the path.

He took out his pen-knife, and prised the thing open. An ancient volume covered in mildewed vellum lay there. He opened it cautiously, apprehensive of what the contents would reveal. There were no intelligible illustrations; the parchment half-rotted pages were penned in hand-writing that had no relationship to any language Adam knew. But he was aware with sudden shocked clarity that the signs and lettering were obscene in the foulest sense possible—anti-God hieroglyphics that filled him with unspeakable terror and aversion.

What lay before him, he knew, was the

penned philosophy of Satanism. In a flash his brain was clarified. The obscene book must have lain buried for centuries, ever since the evil little priest of the Dark Ages had lusted after the young witch. The foul pages were the basis of his unregenerate teaching and would remain so until they were irrevocably destroyed, polluting the very soil of their hiding place. How much the condemned woman had partaken in his vile rituals, no one would ever know. One fact was clear and according to history books proven—she had repulsed and denied him, and consequently met a terrible death through his testimony against her, in the name of religion.

What could be more basely sacrilegious than that? No wonder the vile emanation had remained for so many years befouling the earth, lingering round the deserted shell of a building and the three wretched elders with such intensity.

All the elements of future evil had been ready prepared for Manfred Hearne's malpractice—an influence so concentrated he had been able to conjure it up by will for his own warped ends, like the threads of some gigantic poisonous spider resurrected and drawn from darkness to a vortex of corrupting power.

Magswikk, the village itself, had escaped, because it lay directly outside his pattern. The church was its own guardian. But the wood!—

and the terrain surrounding Summerhayes—those few acres were his objective.

'And my God!' Adam thought, with renewed repulsion, how nearly Hearne had won.

Even as facts slipped into place, his head swam. He stood for a moment or two half swaying, feeling a creeping nauseous ache over his eyes. Then he pulled himself together, took his lighter from a pocket, clicked it and held the flame to a corner of the open pages. At first nothing would burn. Then, suddenly there was a splutter and crackle, a blackening of the sheets followed by a spurt of leaping greenish fire that increased rapidly as whining cries intensified to high pitched screams, bellowing in a frenzied protest through the thickening air. As the scorched pages eventually crumbled into charred dust, it seemed to him great bat-like shapes of darkness descended and enveloped him.

Then, after a timeless interlude, it was over.

How long he stood motionless watching the handful of charred embers caught up on a sudden waft of rising wind, Adam didn't know. But when thought started to register once more he was aware of a developing peace encompassing the plot of ground, as though after long vilification the earth was at last being purified and set free of evil.

Presently he turned, and taking a side path past the house, returned to his car. He drove it a short way nearer to Magswikk, then got out and walked to the village shop.

Eliza Trewartha was arranging a row of paper-back romantic novels on a shelf when he went in. Something in his appearance must have shocked her.

'Why!' she exclaimed. 'Whatever's the matter? Are you all right, surr?'

'In wind and limb, I suppose,' Adam answered. 'I've been hurrying, that's all.'

'Oh—well, in that case—' she continued eyeing him doubtfully before continuing. 'What can I do for you?'

'I'd like a packet of envelopes,' Adam said, on the spur of the moment. 'Two perhaps. Letter writing is about the only social occupation these days with so many empty houses now on the common.'

'Yes, I heard everyone'd taken off,' the woman said pursing her lips. 'Can't say I blame them, but then they shouldn've come in the first place, shu'ld they?—Not *theer*!'

Adam eyed her reflectively as she went to a drawer and took out the envelopes. What did she know he wondered, about past events and the history of the vicarage? Wanting to draw her out, but not wishing to rouse her suspicions, he said, 'I can quite understand that if you *have* to have visitors in the district it's important they should be the right kind. Cornwall is noted for attracting eccentrics and if I were in your place I'd resent them very much indeed.'

'Would you now!' she said unbelievingly.

197

'But then you're one of them, aren't you, surr? And considerin' your poor wife was took along of those others et seems strange to me you should still be about these parts. Excuse me for criticizin', I'm sure. But all the same—' she broke off, eyeing him critically, almost with a glint of fear, her mouth drawn down disapprovingly.

Adam didn't reply at once, then he agreed, 'You're quite right. Nobody can be expected to understand my motives—'

'Oh, I didn' say *that*. They understand all right, or think they do. That woman—Miss Aleyne what's-her-name—?'

Adam flushed.

'I'd rather you left her out of it, if you don't mind. We're leaving as soon as my business is completed here. And I *have* business, Mrs Trewartha.'

'Oh?'

'Yes.'

'And that es, if I may ask?'

'Evidence,' Adam replied cryptically.

'Like a p'liceman, you do sound.'

'In a way perhaps. And however much you disapprove of me—you must know—all Magswikk must know—that wrong things have been going on here for a long time. Evil things that should be stopped. Well, I'm trying to help. That's all.'

'I see.'

'I hope you believe me.'

198

'If you do say so, I s'pose I must,' she said grudgingly. 'I remember you talked about books—history and such like when you first came in here. Did you get what you wanted anywhere?'

'A tour of the libraries helped,' Adam answered. 'The rector wasn't at all forthcoming though. In fact he seemed rather—hostile.'

'The *rector*?' Eliza looked and sounded surprised. 'Oh, I wouldn't've thought that. Such a friendly man he is generally.'

When Adam didn't reply she said, 'I suppose you *do* mean Mr Willis, surr?'

'I didn't ask his name. In fact very little was said between us. On my first visit I was invited in for a few moments and got the impression that the gentleman liked to keep himself very much to himself.'

'Oh, Mr Willis isn't at *all* like that,' the woman said. 'Most friendly, generally. Of course perhaps he'd had a busy day. He has two parishes to look after you know, an' the curate edn' always there—'

'*Two* parishes, did you say?'

She nodded. 'Magswikk an' Gwynesk. And his wife edn' a well person, poor woman.'

'Oh—I see. I didn't realise the rector was a married man,' Adam remarked casually. 'The house seemed to lack any sign of a woman. Rather a dreary place I thought, *dank* and dark, and far too large. But of course in the past rectories were often like that.'

'*Dank? Large?*' Mrs Trewartha almost gasped. 'But my dear soul! It's a *new* building compared to others. Built only 'bout twenty years ago. Before that the last rector had to come two miles of a Sunday from Zillan, why—' her eyes turned suddenly to the window, 'there he is, Mr Willis himself, walking across the green.'

Adam followed her glance and saw some fifty or so yards away a tall thin figure wearing the traditional clergyman's black, striding up the road.

After a considerable pause Adam said, 'I was mistaken then, in thinking I'd met the rector. And I must have called at the wrong house.'

'What do you mean?' Eliza asked with an undertone of fear in her voice.

'I took it that the rectory was that large building directly facing the church.'

The woman's hand went to her mouth as though to smother an exclamation. Then she said, 'But *no one* goes *theer*, surr. *No* one. Bin empty for years an' years. Some say centuries, ever since—' she broke off warily.

'Yes? Ever since what?' Adam prompted her.

'Things happened. That's all I do know,' came the answer, 'bad things.'

'What do you mean by bad? A tragedy of some sort? Murder?'

'Oh no—I didn' say that,' Eliza

200

remonstrated. 'But you know how et is sometimes—stories get about and coloured a bit more each year that passes. Not that I *believe* in them. But I wouldn' put a foot in theer, not for all the tea in China. There've bin a few take over from time to time, like a group of hippies—or squatters if you like—as broke in two years back and plastered notices in the windows. Then one night a young wumman ran out screamin' and was taken off to hospital. The next day they all cleared off. Since then no one's wanted anything to do with the place.'

'Thank you,' Adam said. 'I'm grateful to you for telling me. It's a great help.'

He was at the door on the point of leaving when Eliza asked, 'You say you called there, surr. May I ask what you found?'

Adam tried to reassure her.

'Nothing of importance,' he said ambiguously. 'There was an odd character wandering about, but he soon took off. Probably some crank fancying himself in—Holy Orders.' The words half stuck in his throat, before he continued, 'why hasn't the place been restored or taken down before this?'

'I expec' they was afraid,' Mrs Trewartha answered, turning her face away. 'Some men *did* come—demolishioners I think you call them—round about 1974, but they was frit, and wouldn' continue. So et's been left like that ever since.'

'Oh. I see.'

'Do you, surr?'

'Not completely, Mrs Trewartha, but I think we both agree that any building so riddled with—evil—as that old house is reputed to be, would be better out of the way, and I hope that the authorities will set about it again as soon as possible. I shall certainly see they know my opinions on the matter—' he paused, to smile briefly, before adding '—however much of a busy-body they think me.'

Adam left a minute later, and seeing the rector, Mr Willis, returning down the opposite side of the lane, crossed to meet him. He introduced himself and discovered that what Eliza Trewartha had said was correct. The clergyman was an amiable man, and quite willing—even eager—to discuss the matter of the ancient rectory.

'Due to my calling it isn't advisable for me publicly to express superstitious theories,' he admitted, as they walked slowly on, 'but my private opinion is that the place should certainly be exorcised. My predecessor broached the matter once, but for some reason or other the idea was turned down. So long as no one lives there I suppose no harm is done, and I've done my best to ignore unpleasant stories—which can so easily become exaggerated in county districts. On the whole the inhabitants of Magswikk are healthy minded and actively employed. We have a club, a W.I. and a flourishing little dramatic society. But—'

'Yes?'

'There *is* something wrong there—at the old house—or *has* been, for a very long time. You say you've done a little investigating, well, if you've discovered anything useful I'm grateful. But in view of the recent terrible events round Summerhayes I shall feel bound to put things before the Bishop and local authorities. In any case, from a commonsense point of view the building is an eye-sore.'

Adam agreed, and presently, refusing tactfully, to visit the rector at his cottage for a further chat, he bid him goodbye with a vague promise to call if there was an opportunity later.

Then, after strolling round the village for a bit, he got into his car and started off for home.

*   *   *

The twelve-thirty bus from Penzance was early, and Aleyne started ambling up the lane towards Summerhayes, knowing that she was bound to meet Adam in the car. The earlier grey sky was lifting a little, and pale beams of sunlight filtered through the trees across the road, catching the glint of primroses and fronds of young curling bracken, lighting the clumps of blackthorn and wild flowering cherry

203

to frothing beauty among the green.

There was a heady sweetness in the air that raised her spirits suddenly to optimism and a sense of new things ahead. Just for a brief space of time memories of Samain were almost dispelled, though a niggling unacknowledged unreal fear remained.

And then, suddenly, she saw two pin-points of light glistening from under a bush, bright as stars, green as emeralds. With a lurch of her heart she crossed to the side of the lane, bent down and parted the spreading leaves.

A tiny cat lay there staring up at her. A black cat so aged and small it could have been moulded in miniature as an ornament. But it was alive, and breathed, and the look in its green eyes was no longer vicious and wild, but pitiful in its helpless cry for human attention and understanding. As Aleyne's hand went fleetingly to touch the satin smoothness of its triangular head, the jaws opened soundlessly, and she felt such flood of gratitude from the small creature, emotion tightened in her throat.

'Sam,' she whispered, hardly aware of her own words, '*poor* little Sam. You're free now. Free—free—'

The soft young summer breeze echoed with the whisper of her voice; for a second, no longer, the green eyes blazed, and then the tiny head fell back and all was still.

Aleyne lifted the body into her arms, and

held it there until she was quite sure life was at last extinct. Then she placed it gently again under the leaves and bracken, where it lay, not much larger than a full grown mouse, with eyes closed, in its long sleep.

She got up and stood motionlessly for some minutes, while the rapid pulsing of her heart eased; her throat and mouth were dry. She swallowed nervously, trying to get facts straight in her mind—to understand. But logic wouldn't register. The day had become filled with creeping unease. Samain was over and Hearne was gone, she told herself insistently. Then why this lingering mystery? Why, when alone, should she stumble so unwittingly upon that diminutive feline body?—If it *was* feline. Her impulse was to disturb the greenery again, to prove it. The tiny animal *had* once been Sam. She was as sure of it as she was that it was herself, Aleyne, standing half mesmerised at that quiet hour in the lonely lane.

Yes—lonely.

The trees and undergrowth—the fitful light and air, seemed suddenly bereft and encompassed in desolation. With one hand at her throat, she forced herself to move, and after a quick glance back she started hurrying, half running up the slope towards Summerhayes.

It was then she heard the thrum of an engine, and Adam's car turned the bend behind her.

Relief flooded her with a wave of reaction that shook her whole body. He drew up, calling from the open window, 'You're early. Hop in.' Then noticing her white face, 'What's the matter? You look done in. Aleyne—'

'There's something odd down there,' she replied, trying to sound calm. 'Something not—quite right, Adam.'

He frowned. 'Not right? What do you mean?' He put a hand on her arm to steady her. 'Please, darling—has anyone touched you? For heaven's sake, Aleyne—'

She shook her head wildly, 'It's not that. Not that sort of thing at all. But you must *come*, Adam, see for yourself. It won't take long. Just a little way back. *Please.*'

He shrugged. 'Oh, very well. But can't you give me a clue?'

'It's a cat,' she told him as they walked back. 'A very *very* small cat; it looks like—like Sam.'

He laughed jarringly. '*That* wild thing.'

'Oh, but it's not wild,' she said quietly. 'And it wasn't before it—before it died.' There was a pause before she continued, 'It's dead, Adam. And it had such a strange look in its eyes, as though it was grateful. I put it under some leaves. It was all so pathetic somehow. The way it'd *shrunk*—'

Adam glanced at her uncomfortably, then he remarked, 'Aleyne, are you *sure* about that? It's so easy after the shocks we've had lately to let imagination get out of hand. I had a queer

206

experience this afternoon myself. As it happened, it had more than a grain of truth in it, so I mustn't doubt you, I suppose. Not until I've seen for myself. But we've got to aim for common sense now. Well—' his jaw instinctively tightened '—when we get away from here that should be a whole lot easier.'

She didn't reply, and a few seconds later they reached the spot at the side of the lane where she'd laid the small animal.

'It's just here,' Aleyne said, bending down. 'I know the place exactly. Under these leaves, with the bracken leaning over.' She let a hand rest lightly on the greenery before disturbing it. Then she pulled the leaves away gently and made a little exclamation of astonishment.

'But—'

'Nothing,' Adam said. 'There's no cat there, Aleyne.'

'But there was—there *was*,' she protested. 'I left my handkerchief by that stone, do you see? And it was only a minute or two ago. This was the *place*, Adam. I'm *sure*. Absolutely certain.'

She looked up at him with such bewilderment, almost shock, in her eyes, that he pulled her to her feet and drew her face against his coat. 'Perhaps something took it,' he said, 'a fox or—'

'No, *no*. There wasn't time. Anyway—' she drew herself from his arms and took a second look. 'See—' she cried suddenly, 'there *is* something there.'

They both examined the ground and discovered about half a handful of black fine fur, obviously that of an animal's.

Adam held a piece up between finger and thumb.

'Funny,' he said. 'Now I wonder—' Aleyne rushed to the car. 'Leave it; leave it alone, Adam. I don't want to think of it any more. I don't want to remember,' she cried with a rising note of hysteria in her voice. 'Can't we go away now—tonight? We must get out of it or I shall go mad. I'm mad already I think, I must be—' her voice broke off helplessly.

With his arm round her he tried to soothe her.

'If so, then we both are, my love. Right from the beginning we've experienced these things together. We have to accept events have been abnormal and macabre. Tragic and mysterious, to say the least. But we've weathered them and come out on the other side—'

'*We* have, perhaps, or *may* do. But the others?'

'Get into the car,' Adam said after a short pause. 'Don't think back. It does no good. We've all got things in our lives best forgotten.' His lips tightened, 'Especially, me. Lucinda was my wife, remember? And she's dead. Oh, I don't blame myself or either of us for that. But in retrospect I don't see myself in a particularly commendable light. So for *my* sake as well as yours, will you stop the torturing for a bit?'

She pulled herself together abruptly. 'I'm sorry. I'll try.'

'Good. No one can put the clock back Aleyne. The only thing's to go ahead and make the best of what we've got. And that's quite a bit, isn't it?'

When she didn't answer, he insisted, 'Well, isn't it?' He pressed her hand before starting the engine. Then she turned her head. 'Of course. *Everything.*'

The engine thrummed comfortably up the lane. Superficially the countryside slumbered under a veneer of well-being. Shadows from the pale sunlight quivered across the road from interlaced trees. The burnished glint of a bird's wings almost brushed the windscreen as they neared Summerhayes. The tender green of young leafage was feathered against the clear sky. No trace of recent tragedy marred the landscape; yet both Adam and Aleyne were aware of a faint fear still lingering about the vicinity. Something, Adam told himself, unfinished, which had yet to be concluded. He said nothing to Aleyne of his feelings, but she sensed them.

When the car drew up she said, 'I'd hoped we could get away directly, Adam—perhaps get off tonight. I know it's quick, but—' she sighed, 'but I want to, do you?'

'*Yes,*' he said forcibly, getting out and taking her arm. 'There's nothing I'd like better. But it's not practical.'

209

'Why?'

'There are things to do—tidying up, settling about the post—letters, paying the milk-bill—' he grinned with an attempt at light-heartedness. 'Being a woman you should understand that. Besides—there are surely a few knick-knacks you want to pack and take back with you from the house. That jade figurine you like so much—the paintings—'

'*No.*' Her voice was harsh and strained. 'I don't want a *thing* from this place, Adam, not a single *thing*. When we leave here I want everything to be new and fresh. *Everything.*'

'O.K.,' Adam agreed. 'Just as you say. We'll arrange an auction for later. Leave matters as they are for a time until the sensationalism's died down, then let the auctioneers take over. Things should make quite a packet considering the history of the place.'

'How cynical.'

'Merely realistic, my love. Nothing puts up the price of property and its contents so much as a grim past—especially deaths and murder.'

Aleyne glanced at him quickly. Despite the banter in his voice she knew from a small muscle jerking in his cheek and the set of his jaw he was becoming inwardly on edge.

Just as she was.

But she tried to match up to his assumed mood by saying in forced practical tones, 'Don't exaggerate, Adam. Not *murder* exactly. Mysteries, deaths, yes. But there's a difference

210

isn't there? And after all Summerhayes wasn't exactly in it. It was the wood.'

'I suppose so,' Adam agreed grudgingly.

'But of *course* it was the wood,' Aleyne persisted with more emphasis than was necessary. 'Look, Adam, please try to keep the nastiness away from the house. You say we can't leave tonight, then for heaven's sake, darling, let's be as normal as we can here without having to think about *dying*—' she broke off, ashamed of her own rising nervousness.

He drew her to him gently, kissing her.

'You're right. We're jumpy. That's what it is. Any meal in the offing?'

'It'll have to be salad,' Aleyne told him. 'But there's cold chicken in the fridge, and apple pie.'

'That's fine.'

Aleyne went through to the kitchen, whilst Adam wandered reflectively to the sitting room and poured himself a drink; a stiff one. But it didn't help. The unreasonable impulse was deepening in him that on some pretext or other he had to return to the derelict rectory for a last look round. After his last experience there, commonsense told him there was no cause. The incubus, or whatever it was, of the long dead occupant had been exorcised. He'd watched with his own eyes the unpleasant emanation disintegrate. But—Adam ran a hand through his hair nervously. Why the 'but', he thought irritably. Why on earth have a second thought or doubt about the incident? He hadn't even an excuse to go. No explanation even to conjure up for Aleyne. He could imagine her amazement and dismay if he put the bald truth to her, saying, 'I'm sorry, love, I've just got this thing about a last visit.' Of course he hadn't yet told her the full story. Maybe he wouldn't have to, and *that* would be a relief. Still—realising he was merely wasting time by conjecturing and getting into a muddled maze of his own thoughts, he found a cigarette and felt for the lighter in his coat.

It wasn't there. He searched both pockets, the breast flap and the inner one, but there was no sign of it which was damned annoying, because it was a good one—gold—one of the few valuable mementoes of his father.

While Aleyne was preparing the meal he went to the car and looked thoroughly. Nothing. He was thinking of hurrying back to the spot down the lane where Aleyne had seen the cat when the truth hit him. Of *course*; the probability was that he'd carelessly put the lighter down after burning the odious book, and left it at the rectory.

So he *had* to go back and get it. Fate had supplied him with his excuse after all, just as though the whole thing was intended. The knowledge was a little discomforting, because it endorsed his brooding sense of fatalism—of a *fait-accompli*, though he couldn't say of what.

Even the weather seemed to be changing. In the short time since returning to the house massed clouds had dimmed the sun, and the thin breeze had risen suddenly with a flurrying moan as though a storm was brewing. A rumble of sound came from the distance. Thunder? That was the last thing he'd have expected earlier. Too fresh and spring-like. But then in Cornwall the weather could change unpredictably. So if it was going to rain he'd better nip into the car and have a look for the lighter before the ground was too wet, he thought. He'd be there and back in ten minutes, perhaps less with luck.

He found the table ready laid for the meal, and Aleyne in the kitchen putting finishing touches to the salad. When he told her about the lighter he was surprised by her reaction.

'You're not leaving me alone here, Adam,' she said. 'Not for *one minute*.'

'But I shall be back before you've got your apron off and powdered your nose,' he said. 'It's only a stone's throw away.'

'I don't care,' she insisted stubbornly. 'You haven't told me yet what happened at that beastly place, and if there's anything going on there, I'm going to be in it too—with *you*. Understand?'

Feeling she meant it, he gave in. 'All right; get a coat then, or your cape. Looks to me as though a hell of a storm's coming.'

'Yes.'

As she slipped her light waterproof wrap round her shoulders, she noticed the yellowing heavy sky and lowering of blackish clouds from the direction of Magswikk; and when they got into the car the first few spots of rain were already spattering the windscreen.

'It won't be much yet,' Adam said, as he pressed the accelerator, 'with a bit of luck we'll be back before the worst.'

'What made you put your lighter down there?' Aleyne asked curiously. 'On a stone, you said. What were you doing?'

'I'll explain that later,' he told her a little shortly. 'And I said I *thought* I had, that's all.'

'Sorry I asked,' she said.

He touched her hand lightly. 'Darling, be patient just for a bit,' he pleaded. 'When we're back you shall hear it all. The full story.'

After that they rode on in silence, an interlude for him filled with growing apprehension which intensified into acute dread as they neared the brooding stark shape of the house. The light by then had become thunderous dark brown, streaked with luminous green above the dejected landscape. On the opposite side of the lane the tombstones seemed to lean like living entities warding off assault. Aleyne shivered.

'What a depressing dreary place. Really, Adam—you've got odd tastes sometimes for the macabre.'

Her tones were commonsense, even light.

214

But her mind was not. She had an almost overpowering impulse to jump out of the car and rush back to Summerhayes. Adam too was acutely on edge.

He drew in to the side of the lane and switched off the engine. 'I shall nip down by the side to the back. Will you stay here? It'll only take a minute, and the rain's really starting now.'

'Oh no,' she said. 'Not for one moment.'

'Come along then.'

With the hood of her cape pulled down over her head Aleyne followed him down a dreary path bordered by a few bushes and stunted wind-blown trees. A flurry of leaves was torn from a sycamore and driven to the ground on a rush of rain-thick air as they passed. One caught Aleyne's cheek like the slap of a hand. Involuntarily she gave a little cry.

Adam turned his head sharply, 'What's the matter?'

'Nothing,' she told him, wiping a strand of hair from her eyes. 'A leaf caught me, that's all. How far now?'

'We're here,' Adam told her, cutting abruptly to the left. The back door was creaking from the strengthening impact of the elements as they went by; and underfoot the ground was already sticky from dank wet earth.

'Here we are,' he said, when they reached the end of the straggling path. 'It was somewhere near that stone.' All the time the sky was darkening ominously; there was a further crack of thunder and the rising swish of rain beating the undergrowth.

'Where? Here?' Aleyne asked, looking down. 'I can't see anything.'

Adam drew a torch from his pocket, and switched it on saying, 'Good thing I brought this along. It's like—'

'The end of the world,' Aleyne interrupted before he could finish.

She heard his saying, 'I'm sorry, my love. I *did* tell you to wait in the car.' His hands were searching through weeds and over the surface of stones in the circling light of the torch.

There was nothing.

Aleyne, shivering, pulled her cape more closely round her chin. 'It could be *any*where, Adam,' she couldn't help remarking. 'Along the path or—did you go into the house?'

'Yes, but I'd had no reason to use it there,' Adam answered. 'All the same I'll take a look near the door.'

She followed him to the back entrance where the rotted door gaped and swayed with a curious resemblance of hungry giant jaws in wait. The atmosphere from within smelled unhealthily foetid, penetrating insidiously from the neglected interior to the gusty air outside.

'Don't go in,' Aleyne cried, as Adam pushed the wood. Was it her fancy, or was there immediately the hollow echo of obscene laughter ahead?

216

Adam took her hand. 'I think we must, darling.'

'*Now*?' Her voice was fearful.

The following moment a blinding flash of lightning zig-zagged across the ground and sky, accompanied by a shattering roar of thunder. The rain swept in a merciless torrent against their bent forms.

'Come along.' Adam took her hand, and with one shoulder forced the door open dragging her through. A bat, disturbed, fell with a thud from the passage ceiling. Aleyne screamed.

'It's all right,' he said, pausing to get his breath, 'but the storm's directly overhead. Stick it for a bit, Aleyne. It won't be long—'

But he knew that it was something more than the storm that had driven him into the house—a compulsion and sense of evil still to be faced that had drawn him back to the ancient rectory in the first place. The lighter had been merely incidental.

After a brief pause still with Aleyne's hand in his, he went on again, moving the torch fitfully so its glow lit crumbling walls and cracked floors to sudden clarity that as quickly slipped into shadow again. What made him pause, standing rigidly gripping Aleyne's wrist he never knew. But as they waited motionless in the darkness the thunder started up again, crash after crash, accompanied suddenly by a roaring of falling masonry and timber. Dust and stones were driven in a thick cloud from a gaping structural hole ahead; and Aleyne's free hand went instinctively to her face as an immense ball of fire shattered the roof, rolling and spitting like a living entity towards them. Aleyne, with her eyes hidden, mercifully did not see what Adam did—a momentary leaping curdling form of evil with horned head and wavering grasping arms that became one with the thunder bolt—a satanic emanation bent on human destruction.

Almost simultaneously tongues of flame caught rubble from a corner, shooting forward over the floor in their direction as the brilliant orange claws, lit by lurid green and writhing grey, billowed and spread graspingly, catching at walls and tumbled ancient relics until the whole place was blazing—a roaring inferno of heat and smoke.

Aleyne, choking for air, slumped helplessly against Adam's rasping form. The world seemed to topple round him, as fingered blackened arms clawed maliciously for his neck. A few words of an ancient prayer left his dry lips. Above his head there was a curdling and wavering of two immense reddened eyes which narrowed briefly, then blazed intermittently—dilating and contracting while he summoned sufficient strength and willpower to drag Aleyne back towards the door.

Bricks toppled; rafters fell. There was a

screaming, and groaning, the shrill splintering of wood ending in a drawn-out high-pitched cry of agony followed by a thickened cloud of darkness.

Then, mercifully, a waft of air, as the door shattered and tumbled.

Adam, still with his arms round Aleyne, dragged himself on his knees over the ground. He held her for a moment before other hands reached and took her from the searing heat; then he toppled back, and lay for a minute gasping from constricted lungs, for oxygen and life.

The struggle was short—just as though, in those few seconds, the evil spirit of the house disintegrated and died. Even the rain had stopped. A few local people were on the scene by then, and as he was helped to his feet by a neighbouring farmer, he'd recovered sufficiently to see Aleyne in the distance being cared for by a village woman.

With two strong hands grasping his arm in support, he stumbled over the scorched ground to where she lay, half propped up by the friendly woman. To his relief she appeared unharmed, even managed a smile when he approached.

'Oh, Adam,' she said, 'What a sight I must look—'

'Yes,' he agreed, 'you do.'

It was quite true. Her face was blackened with rivulets of smoky perspiration coursing

219

from forehead and nose to chin, straggling hair tangled with dust and dirt, yet sodden from the storm. 'What a way to talk,' the kindly woman chided her, helping her to her feet. 'Lucky to be alive you are. As if anyone do care how you *look*. That's vanity for 'ee, all right.'

*   *   *

Several hours passed before the fire was finally extinguished, and most of the night a dull glow hovered over the blackened site. Even at Summerhayes the smell of burning lingered in the air, blown insidiously on the dying wind.

By morning, after a period of fitful sleep all seemed comparatively quiet again. Any sounds to be heard were those of nature—young birds chortling from their nests, the clatter of a farm cart along the lane, and distant call of a cuckoo from over the wood somewhere.

'Listen, Adam,' Aleyne said, as she brought coffee to the lounge. 'The first cuckoo.'

Haunting and predictive of summer ahead, its mocking voice flooded the air. Aleyne threw the window wide. 'And look—' she said, 'the blossom's out.'

It was true.

During a few hours the wild cherry had burst from bud into a foam of white against a clear blue sky.

Adam took her hand, holding it tight.

'Let's take it as a promise, love,' he said,

'And hope for the future.'

'Yes,' she agreed. 'It will be all right, Adam. I'm sure it will.'

Later that day they learned on Radio News that Manfred Hearne, a central figure in the sensational Magswikk affair, had been found dead from a fit at the mental home where he was detained. A curious fact was that he appeared also to be burned about the face and hands which was odd, as no matches or inflammable objects were allowed in his possession.

Investigations, it was stated, were in process. Aleyne and Adam looked at each other. They said nothing, but it was obvious to both that the mystery would never rationally be solved.

But then neither would that of the three elders which had so curiously withered and shrunk during the fire. They had been far enough away from the holocaust to escape any material scorching. None of the other trees or undergrowth nearby had suffered. The curious fact remained, however, that after centuries of growth and withstanding the elements, they had suddenly crumbled into decay, each morning diminishing in size until only short blackened stumps remained.

When summer came even these were gone and nothing remained to indicate they had ever stood there. Young green quickly covered the site so long corrupted by an evil past. Life and health returned to the area which was eventually taken over by the authorities as a nature reserve and bird sanctuary.

The residential houses were demolished, as it was discovered the drainage had been wrong, giving rise to unhealthy gases in the area.

Birds now sing where once Manfred Hearne's insidious melody filled the air. The feet of small wild creatures patter along the hidden paths of Bran's domain.

As for Bran?

But who can say? He is already forgotten except by the few who knew him.

We hope you have enjoyed this Large Print book. Other Chivers Press or Thorndike Press Large Print books are available at your library or directly from the publishers.

For more information about current and forthcoming titles, please call or write, without obligation, to:

Chivers Press Limited
Windsor Bridge Road
Bath BA2 3AX
England
Tel. (01225) 335336

OR

Thorndike Press
P.O. Box 159
Thorndike, Maine 04986
USA
Tel. (800) 223-2336

All our Large Print titles are designed for easy reading, and all our books are made to last.